A BARGAIN FOR BLISS

Book Two of the Raven Court Chronicles

AUTUMN WOLFF

This is a work of fiction. Names, characters, business, events and incidents are the products of the author's imagination. Any resemblance to actual persons, living or dead, or actual events is purely coincidental.

Cover design by HowlAtTheMoon

First Kindle paperback edition: July 2023

DEDICATION

This book is dedicated to my wife, Meghan, who passionately supports all the wild words I slap down on the page. It's also dedicated to the girls who are practically my little sisters at this point, Layn and Kare Bear. All three are very dear to me in ways my words alone cannot express.

CHAPTER ONE

I heard her before she entered the room. Her footsteps were light as if the wind carried her feet across each piece of the floor. And sometimes it actually did. She used to sneak up on me, but in the three months I'd lived in Featherstone, the Raven Queen had fallen prey to my advanced predatory senses, the kind only a fierce huntress could cultivate.

My senses would never be as sharp as those of my inner wolf, but enough bled through our connection that I was a better tracker than any human and most faeries.

Casually striding over to the window in my bedroom, I unlatched it and waited for the queen's knock at my door. The monarch knocked exactly twice. She was growing impatient.

Good, I thought. Just what I wanted.

I called for my mistress to enter, and she opened the door. I noticed Barsilla, her arrogant left-hand lady hovering just above the queen's shoulder. That piskie had grown increasingly fed up with my antics as of late. At least, she made a big show of it.

Of course, when my eyes hovered over the queen, I felt

my heart skip a beat. Eyes widening as though I was looking at her for the first time, I came within inches of dropping my plan entirely. Her otherworldly beauty held me in a trance, seven feet of alluring artistry from her sleek obsidian hair to her enrapturing violet eyes. They held all the mysteries of a Faerie Queen seemingly within range, daring all who saw to reach forward.

Her words floated across the room to my ears with all the confidence of a monarch who expected obedience and steadfast loyalty.

"Come, my pet. I'm scheduled to hold court in 10 minutes, and I need my fearsome beast."

It took almost everything I had not to prance across the room and throw myself at her. The tiny fae hovering nearby had her usual pencil and clipboard out at the ready in case she needed to write down something important. Barsilla's eyes practically said, "Do it. I dare you."

But that was ridiculous. The piskie couldn't have known what I was planning, right? I looked at Barsilla again in her tiny librarian outfit. And just staring at the representation of order and rules in the palace rekindled some spark of rebellion in my bratty ass.

"Apologies, mistress," I said, not looking at Varella again because I knew her eyes would lure me in again, freezing me in my tracks.

"Don't you dare," was all I heard Barsilla say as I frantically slid the window open and leaped outside. The queen was fast, and I felt her grasp millimeters from my nape as I dove toward the palace grounds a few stories below.

Landing and immediately tucking into a roll, I exhaled. Then I rose with as much speed as I could leech from my inner wolf and bolted toward the back of Featherstone.

From the window, I heard my mistress' low tenor voice

carry a warning, "My pet. . ."

Those words sent a shiver down my spine, and I knew this was fucking with her schedule. But I didn't care. You welcome a brat into your home, and you should anticipate the consequences.

I didn't hear her leaping out the window after me, just the soft swish of wild rye grass under my feet as I bolted away.

Will she endure the humiliation of being seen chasing down her pet werewolf, or will the mighty queen march herself to hold court without the fierce beast she's grown so accustomed to wielding over her nobles and guests? I thought, snickering.

A few months ago when I'd arrived at Featherstone, freshly ensnared in a bargain of the queen's making, I wouldn't have dared acted this way. There were probably mice in the walls of the basement that were less timid than me.

But what can I say? The queen and her best intelligence agent had made me very comfortable here. They'd given the werewolf a cookie, and in turn, she'd not only stolen the entire glass of milk but the jar of remaining sweets as well.

Okay, normally I wasn't this bad. But this week had been long, and restlessness was building up in every joint of my body. Maybe I was a little pissy.

The rear guard tower came into view as I rounded a corner.

It stood a few stories higher than my window with a narrow spiral staircase running up the center. A few faerie guards stood on the ground watching me bolt for the stone bridge behind the palace. They were armed with spears and leather armor bearing the queen's crest in the center, a black bird, head back, beak open, and crying to the sky with its wings spread wide.

The guards looked nervously at each other as I continued running full speed in nothing but my silk pajamas with various puppy designs sewn into the fabric. My curly brown hair bounced behind me, and I realized the guards were calculating how much trouble they'd get in if I was allowed to simply cruise on by.

"Um. . . Sierra?" A guard with short green hair cut into a bob stammered as she took a step to block my path.

I leaped about five feet over her head using every bit of that borrowed werewolf strength in my legs. She didn't move to grab me, scratching her cheek in confusion. Looking further up the guard tower, she called for Ceras.

The queen's top talon jumped from the second story and landed behind me, hand axe rattling at their side.

"What is it, Belamie?" They asked as I continued running for the bridge, morning sunlight reflecting off the lake. The scent of forest and fish hit my senses as I realized that I was nearly free.

"Do we just let the royal pet go?" Belamie asked.

Turning back for a brief moment and running in reverse, I yelled, "Ceras! If you see the queen, stall her! And suggest to her that I went out the front gate into town. Please and thank you!"

Rushing off into the tree line, the last thing I heard was Ceras chuckling to themselves and stretching.

"Patrols turn up anything this morning?" They asked.

"No," Belamie said.

"Then we'll let her majesty sort out this issue with her pet. She'll be fine," Ceras said. "Besides, I doubt the queen has let her prized possession get too far ahead of her."

Rushing into the trees and seeing aspens, evergreens, and other greenery native to Faerie, I sneered.

Bullshit, I thought. There's no way the queen would

delay court to rush after me.

Bushes whipped around me, and I jumped over a stump, knowing it would be more difficult for the queen to fly through the treetops and snatch me from above. That was assuming she was giving chase.

After about five minutes, I came to a stop, sweaty and heart-hammering. This particular patch of trees wasn't far from where the queen had put down my inner wolf, earning the right to be my pack leader.

My eyes darted at every snapped twig, a bead of sweat running down my cheek. To my left, a rabbit took one look at me and decided it could afford the risk of chomping on a purple flower nearby.

Bitch, I'm a werewolf, I thought. You should be fleeing in the opposite direction.

Puffing out my chest, I turned toward the brown and white rabbit. I put my hands on my hips and said, "Excuse me. Do you know what I am? You dare to snack in the presence of a fearsome werewolf? An apex predator, for which, capturing a rabbit in her jaws would be pup's play?"

The rabbit didn't even turn its head to acknowledge my words. It just continued chewing on the flower's stem, taking the vegetation in like a board into a sawmill.

Raising my hands slowly and pretending I had the claws of my inner wolf, I took a step toward the bunny.

"You should be more cautious in assessing your surroundings for danger, Bugs."

The rabbit's blue eyes finally glanced over at me as it sniffed at another flower nearby, this one with a large yellow bulb. Its nose and whiskers twitched before it decided to ignore me once more and snatch another snack.

"I'm serious, little bunny. Surely you smell the wild

canine inside of me. Your heart should be pounding in your chest, eyes watching my claws for any hint of movement. Otherwise, when you're distracted, you might find yourself suddenly hoisted into the air and EEEEEP—," I shrieked, interrupted by a sudden, terrible force of upward movement that snagged my shoulders.

Up through tree branches I went, air sucked out of my lungs from sheer terror at the speed I was being carried.

Looking down, I watched the trees below me start to shrink, and then I felt myself suddenly reversing direction, falling toward the lake approaching terminal velocity.

"Fuuuuuccccckkkk meeeeeeee," I screamed, preparing for a sudden bath of epic proportions. As a werewolf, I was a bit tougher than the average human, even when I walked on two legs. But from this height, I could at least expect a bruise or two landing in the water.

And then, just as I steadied myself for a fishy fate, a pair of well-toned arms caught me just a few feet above the lake water. I was close enough to already smell the algae and aquatic turtles I prepared to join. Yet, I'd been given a reprieve.

Looking up at my savior, I saw the Raven Queen grinning down at me with all the smug satisfaction radiating from her face that she could muster. Two large black-feathered wings carried us over the water as Varella gradually moved into a hover, holding me Lois Lane style in her arms.

The lake wind swirled around my hair and floppy pajamas as her violet eyes found mine. The inhuman red eyes I carried were locked in her gaze, not even wielding enough strength to frighten a wee rabbit. Goddamn, some days I was a downright disgrace to the canine race.

"Well, my pet. I hope you got all those. . .what do you mortals call them? Zoomies? Out of your system. We've got a long day at court ahead," she said, the grin never leaving her face. She knew I wouldn't get far. She knew!

Sighing, I crossed my arms.

"I bet I was so close to getting away. You probably panicked and used all your magic to track me down," I said, frowning.

"Actually, I was watching you from the sky the entire time. You're in the heart of my court, where my magic is at the epicenter of intensity. Before your feet even touched the ground I was in the air above you," she said, laughing.

Her dulcet chortle left me wanting to curl up in her arms and wrap myself tightly within her grip, closing my eyes and forgetting about all the needs and responsibilities of running a queendom for the day.

But no! I'd done this for a reason, and she needed to know why. Even if the inconvenience was beyond minor, she had to know there was a point. Well. . .as much of a point as my bratty ass could make for being obstinate, which typically wasn't much beyond being eternally difficult for the sake of adversity.

"Yeah, well. I wasn't even really trying. You're lucky I didn't let my inner wolf loose," I said, arms crossed tighter.

"Ah yes, an ability you've yet to manifest here, even after three full moons. But rest assured, my pet. Even if you were on four paws instead of two legs, I could have easily snatched you from the forest floor as I did just minutes ago," she said.

And then the queen's grin started to fade as she raised an eyebrow.

"Though your inner wolf wouldn't have run just before court anyway. It seems to be tamer the longer you remain under the weight of my sorcery and influence, bound by my bargain. But you, Sierra, acted out unexpectedly this morning. Why?"

This was my chance! Here I could let her have it! But instead of unleashing a torrent of words, I just found myself lost in her eyes again. There wasn't an ounce of impatience in her voice, despite today's events being delayed by a few minutes. Though, I guess you start court when the queen says you start court. And if you have a complaint, her werewolf would bite your face off.

Sighing again, I sagged in her grip, words caught in my throat that I couldn't seem to dislodge or cough up. Fuck, all I could do was that infamous bottom gesture where I pointed my index fingers at each other and looked pathetic.

On second thought, it's no wonder the rabbit didn't run away screaming earlier, I thought.

"Come now, my pet. You ran for a reason. Out with it. It's just the two of us here over the lake," Varella said with an added softness to her tone. The game was over. And now I had to suffer the consequences of my actions, namely being upfront about my feelings. Surely there was something a little easier I could endure, being locked in an Iron Maiden or forced to listen to Rascal Flatts on repeat?

The queen made no move to rush me, which just increased the feelings of wanting to curl up tight against her breasts and have a few hours with her all to myself.

"You've been so busy lately," I finally managed in a pathetic whisper. That was all the queen got for at least 30 seconds.

A crane covered in pink and white feathers flew around us and closer to the shoreline of the palace while my mistress waited for more words.

"And Lily's still gone on her assignment in the Tulip Court. I just — maybe I needed you to pay attention to your pet for a few minutes this morning," I said, looking anywhere but her eyes. Saying this stuff was embarrassing enough.

The Raven Queen did not sigh. And she chose her following words carefully.

"You speak right, my little wolf. My work and duties have increased threefold over the last few weeks," she said.

"And you won't tell me what you've been working on. Whenever I ask, you give me some vague answer meant to dismiss my curiosity," I said.

The queen looked over the palace for a moment. Her eyes carried a quiet contemplation that I couldn't begin to analyze. But then again, she was a Faerie Queen who'd lived for centuries. Her perspective was bound to be drastically different from mine. And maybe I'd forgotten that.

"I've been working on Bliss, Sierra. And it's remained under wraps so much so that not even Ceras knows about it. So, why don't we have dinner tonight, just the two of us, and then I'll finally answer all your questions," the queen said.

Now that did lift my heart pretty high to the point I felt like I was running on clouds. Damn if my mistress didn't know exactly what strings to pull.

All I could do was nod and finally give in to the temptation to nuzzle up into Varella. I breathed deep in her scent of chilly night air and raspberries that I'd come to associate with safety and comfort. I sighed one last time, content with the answers that'd been given me.

The Raven Queen leaned down and slowly kissed my forehead, sending a tickle of delirium through my mind. It was something much more powerful than serotonin, and I made a muffled noise of pleasure.

"Can we head back to Featherstone now? I'm afraid your inner wolf's presence is required," Varella whispered.

"Just one more minute hovering here, please. I need you, mistress. So let me have you for just a little longer."

And because she spoiled me rotten, I got five more minutes with Varella just holding me over the water, morning breeze carrying our hair around us this way and that.

I need to run away from her more often, I thought.

CHAPTER TWO

The announcement sounded like always, "Announcing Queen Varella, ruler of the Raven Court at Featherstone, she who soars high above and wields the Dark Wind. And her pet, the Wolf of Featherstone."

After my inner girl helped defend the palace against an invasion from the lake, our title received a promotion.

Hushed whispers became the norm for me after I arrived in court. The nobles never seemed to tire of looking at the queen's pet werewolf. Covered from head to tail in walnut-colored fur, weighing over 200 pounds, and carrying a jaw of teeth strong enough to pull apart iron bars, I was the perfect beast for the bird lady to tut around and keep others in line.

When the queen sat at her emerald-encrusted throne carved from stone and covered in cawing ravens, I joined her. Some days she wanted me closer and others further. But I was always in the chair with her.

The damn thing was big enough to hold three people. But the Raven Queen and her werewolf filled it comfortably. This particular morning the queen lightly tapped her left leg with two fingers, a movement I'd been careful to watch for over the last few months.

That meant she wanted my paws and head strewn across her lap. So I obliged. Because she was my pack leader, and my devotion to her was absolute. Though that certainly wasn't the case when I first arrived after finding the inner girl had willingly ensnared herself in the queen's service.

I tried my best facing off against the Raven Queen in the forest not far from here. To her credit, she gave me a fair shot. But I wasn't nearly fast or strong enough to put her down. The feeling of being flipped over and slammed into the dirt hard enough to rattle trees around me was something I had trouble forgetting.

Looking out at the gathered nobles, faeries of the Raven Court who had assembled to speak before the queen or witness those who were, I saw more apprehension than normal. A goblin covered in blue flesh and wearing the fanciest rainbow suit I'd ever seen was sweating up a storm. A pair of mated centaurs were shuffling in place, hoves lightly clopping on the stone floor, cotton dresses swaying gently with their movements. On the opposite wall, a girl with the wings of a butterfly twiddled her thumbs, something that, until now, I'd assumed was just what my inner girl called an "expression."

Random nobles cleared their throats, coughed a little, and wiped their foreheads, waiting for the queen to speak.

My pack leader remained silent, observing her people, trying to figure out what had them all so jittery. Or maybe she already knew. Her mouth revealed neither a smile nor a frown. Varella's eyes retained their frosty gare.

After ruling this court for centuries, the dark monarch of Faerie learned to keep a tight grip on everything going on inside her thoughts and feelings. And on the off chance something slipped through, I was here to steal attention from the witnesses so they'd miss whatever nugget the queen might've dropped.

"Let the queen's business commence," she said at once and without warning. "I believe we have a long list of petitioners this day. No sense in dallying. Whoever is first to address me, step forth."

The hushed whispers came to a stop as soon as she'd gotten a single word out. All eyes were turned toward the space in front of the throne. More cawing from the ravens on the back of Varella's giant chair filled the chamber as we waited for the first person to take their place before the queen.

"I will approach the throne to start today's business if it pleases you, my queen," an individual called from the tightest cluster of nobles. They stood near the large brass doors at the entrance of the throne room. And I watched that group clear out as quickly as their legs would carry them when this faerie spoke.

My pack leader motioned with two fingers for the speaker to come closer.

Approaching the throne with a cautious demeanor, hands folded together as though one or both might run away if not held tight, an androgynous individual stopped about 15 feet before the queen. I raised my head to get a better look at the faerie that smelled of lemongrass and peppermint.

Their orange hair was pulled back into a braid that swiveled back and forth on their approach. Brown eyes that couldn't help but find their way down to me once in a while watched the queen for any sign of immediate displeasure. This individual's movements were all carefully measured, as if every toe that made contact with the ground only did so after days of nonstop planning.

It went beyond the otherworldly grace that typically accompanied faeries who danced along the shores of eternity as though it were as natural a thing as breathing or blinking.

This elf was tall and willowy, dressed in a well-tailored black vest covered in silver star designs. A short-sleeved white button-down shirt was tucked into their dark trousers, which were also decorated with silver stars and even bigger constellations.

"Who addresses me?" the queen asked, her tone warming a little bit.

They took a moment to gather their breath before speaking. Another quaint calculation on their part, eyes circling back around to me for just a moment.

"My name is Dareth Ickmunt. I bring you a petition from the Court of Stars, your grace," they said, bowing their head.

A smile danced on the corner of Varella's lips, and I looked from her back over to Dareth. The petitioner did not speak another word until the queen had time to consider their identity.

"Ickmunt. . . surname of the Star Court ruler. It's been some time since I've spoken with King Falmouth Ickmunt. Of course, everyone knows he has no living sons. But I've heard he keeps a nephew close at hand, even granted him the title of prince. So tell me Prince Dareth, why do you visit my court without an official announcement? Foreign royalty doesn't typically approach my throne among the nobles during court."

Dareth paused and considered their next words. They made no effort to hide their identity. Now that I got a better look at the prince, I saw a blue crescent moon tattooed on their neck, along with more stars marking their terra-cotta flesh. It was intricate inkwork and truly set them apart from even the nobles.

"Forgive me, your grace. I did not mean to deceive you. Nor have I come to your court sans announcement for the purpose of spycraft or war. I only wear the title of 'prince' to placate my uncle. He is anxious about succession, you see. But I've never considered myself royalty, despite his decree," they said.

Varella clicked her tongue.

"So you come to my court without using a title for the sake of humility?" my pack leader asked.

"It is as you say, your grace. I am not one for putting on airs. I find they needlessly devour my time," the prince said.

They seemed to have found their noble legs, speaking a little more forcefully now, not with any aggression, just more surety. The elf may not want a title, but I saw nobility within their inflection now. It was their eyes, those locked with the pupils of my pack leader. Each knew who they were dealing with now. No games. Just the queen's business.

My ears twitched as I heard the nobles whispering amongst themselves once more.

"The Court of Stars? Why would their prince travel this far south?"

"I'm not sure I like the sound of this unannounced royalty."

"Why come here to our court if not to bring trouble? I don't like his timing or tidings."

They continued to speak in hushed voices, but I tuned out and focussed once more on Dareth as the queen raised an eyebrow.

"You speak of your time as though you have any. Our kind does not carry burdens brought on by the strands of time as mortals do. So, it's a curious thing to hear you speak of it in such a way," shc said.

With their eyes sharpened, the prince said, "You and I may have a ladle that can be dipped into the well of ages without limit, but my court faces the end of its days. This is why I come here to petition you, your grace."

Her amusement was gone. My pack leader's stare had grown cold again. I had only run in this world for a few months, but these were Faerie courts being spoken of now. Centuries of time wound up in each through peace and conflict. It was simply beyond the mind of me or my inner girl. Such was the comprehension of mortals and beasts.

"The Court of Stars is in danger of collapse?" the queen asked.

The prince nodded.

"My home of 90 years faces invasion, if not utter annihilation, from the Fist of Kairn, an alliance of courts who've expanded their military presence in neighboring territories far to the north. My uncle remains convinced our pacifism will keep us safe, and that the stain of dishonor that would come from taking a peaceful court will be enough deterrence. But I remain unconvinced."

It wasn't just whispering now from the nobles. A few of them were starting to speak at full volume.

"I knew it! He's come here to drag us into war."

"Surely they can't expect us to protect them from so far away. That's absurd."

"I say we ransom the prince off to the Fist of Kairn here and now. Then we avoid war and bring in a little coin."

That last suggestion elicited a growl from yours truly. It was enough that the court came to a pause. When a wolf growls, the grotto takes notice. When a werewolf growls, the entire forest takes notice.

But my pack leader was not looking around the room to survey expressions from her people. She remained hyperfocused on the prince who'd traveled so far to be here, chased by the threat of war.

"Your uncle is an optimistic king. I will not speak ill of him, but his decision and confidence in honor seem precarious. So tell me, Prince Dareth, what exactly have you traveled all this way to ask me? What request was important enough that it had to be delivered in person and could not risk being sent via crow messenger?"

Another deep breath from Dareth before he spoke.

At the throne's top, each raven perched silently, almost as if they were made of stone like the chair we sat in.

"You spent some years growing up in the Court of Stars, your grace. We still have a large painting of you and your brother when you were just a girl, studying constellations and the movement of celestial bodies with my aunt and uncle. I've come here to ask that if war were to swallow my home, you be prepared to receive fleeing refugees."

Varella considered this, crossing her legs and placing both of her hands on top of my head, which found itself in her lap once more.

"You're not asking me to intervene militarily but to be ready to welcome evacuees should the Fist of Kairn bring destruction to your doorstep?" my pack leader clarified.

"My uncle has forbidden requests for defensive aid, citing our court's laws. Pacificism means that not only do we avoid fighting, but our court refuses to allow others to fight for us. So I've come here to seek the next best thing. I made similar requests to the Yellow Court and Worm Court, but they turned me down almost immediately," Dareth said.

I picked up the sound of footsteps as a noble stepped

into view behind Dareth. He was a sturdy man wearing a red robe with gold trim. It covered most of his alabaster skin. The fae's black hair was cut short, and his yellow eyes washed over the prince from behind.

"My queen, you cannot grant the prince's petition. The Raven Court would risk further ire from the Star Court's enemies if we welcomed survivors of a hypothetical calamity. Our resources are—"

The Raven Queen cut him off.

"I'm well aware of our resources, Lord Kitac. I do sit this throne and manage this court each week, do I not? So why would you presume to tell me things I already know? Or would you accuse your ruler of being ignorant of her queendom's assets?"

I didn't give Lord Kitac time to respond, rising to my feet and leaping down from the throne to the stone floor. My large paws passed over gemstones in the landing beneath me. I strode past Dareth, not paying him a lick of attention. My fur came within inches of their legs.

My haunches popped as I assumed my full height and might, gradually approaching the lord who spoke out of turn.

Even though the other nobles were nowhere near my path, they backed up against the wall as I passed. Their heartbeats were growing faster. And why? They'd seen this play out before with Lord Harroldsen. They watched as I tore his throat open in an instant.

But not here. I took my time approaching this lord so he could stew in the juices of this particular error.

Lord Kitac was a man of average height, but I watched him start to shrink before my very eyes upon my approach. He made no move to run, and it was just as well. Outrunning a werewolf was not a common feat.

A deep, echoing growl resonated across the throne

room. I watched as his face sank with each second that noise rattled in his ears. The confidence he so boldly spoke with just seconds ago had taken a sudden leap into a bottomless chasm. And I suspected he now wished his body could do the same.

I had a job to do here. My pack leader is a terrifying monarch. But she doesn't have to put her power on display every time she sits the throne. If a ruler had to show their true power very often, they wouldn't have a court to manage for long. That's where I came in. Because a wolf can be terrifying each time you see one.

And a werewolf? Well, folks didn't even need to see us to be afraid. A lone snarl echoing from the dark is enough to make most folks turn tail and run, especially when they so effortlessly felt the rumble penetrating deep into their core.

I could be the threat and power flexed every day without a single noble questioning the strength of my queen. That's why I'm here. I am her beast. The queen has her talons, her beak, her Dark Wind, and through me, she has claws and jaws that could fell any number of enemies.

Flashing fangs, I padded another step closer to Lord Kitac, and any surety he had left dove into the same chasm that he wanted to hide in at this very moment.

The noble fell to his knees and folded his hands.

"Mercy, please, your grace. I spoke out of turn. Please forgive me. Of course you know the resources of this court. You surely do," the man said, nodding as if to convince himself.

Before I could step closer, my pack leader called for me.

"That's enough, my pet. Lord Kitac knows he fucked up. Come back to me," she said.

I locked eyes with the sweating fae noble for what felt

like several minutes before turning to leave. He fell to his ass catching his breath and then slowly stood, trying to gravitate to a section of the wall where everyone would forget he existed.

As I climbed back onto the throne, the Raven Queen stroked my neck and said, "Good girl. Such a fearsome beast you are."

I let my tongue hang out for a moment before locking eyes with Dareth and resuming a more vigilant pose.

My pack leader stood and addressed, not just the prince, but her gathered nobles now.

"You who call the Raven Court home, I do not blindly ignore your fears and worries. Whispers of war to the north have grown louder these last few weeks. And now that we have a physical reminder of that conflict before our eyes, I understand why it makes you uneasy," she said.

Dareth said not a word. He stood listening to my pack leader with a calm demeanor that did not once lead me to believe he felt ignored by the queen's change of attention.

"This court has seen war. We've seen death. But I will remind you that in my centuries on this throne, not once have I dragged our people into battle unjustly. Aggressors have tried their hand at conquering us, and enemies have stood at the gates of Perth before! Some of you were here to witness that. And what did I do?"

The hypothetical question was accompanied only by ravens above me, summoning their chorus of caws again.

Nobody answered the queen.

"I soared over those gates and struck down our enemies with a feathered blade in each hand. Time and time again, I have rallied our talons and feathers to drive the enemy back. You know me. I do not pick fights with other courts, and I do not loan our military to be a strength for others unless required to do so by established treaties. Do you not recall mere months ago when I avoided embroiling us in a war between the Yellow Court and Worm Court? Have you all forsaken belief in my wisdom so easily?"

Now some nobles did answer her.

"No!"

"We believe in you, our queen!"

"You've not failed us one single day on that throne."

My pack leader nodded to her nobles. The energy in the room had completely changed. She'd whipped up their confidence into a fervor, all with a few words. I rose from the throne and stood at her side, my shoulders in line with her hips.

"You trusted me then. I call upon you to also believe in me now. I will not summon the ire and war of northern kingdoms to these lands. The Raven Court will remain safe and prosperous as it has for many years. So I ask you all, here and now, do you trust your queen?"

And with a thunderous echo, each lord and lady present hollered in affirmation.

"Armed with your confidence, I will continue to protect our lands. I appreciate you all," my pack leader said.

Turning toward the prince as the nobles talked excitedly amongst themselves, the Raven Queen had softer words.

"Prince Dareth, I invite you to stay here at Featherstone tonight as my guest. If you accept my invitation, then we'll discuss your request for prepared aid in the morning."

The fae prince bowed.

"I appreciate your hospitality and am happy to accept, your grace."

My pack leader awarded him a brief nod and then

resumed her seat on the throne, calling me to her once more.

"Come now, my pet. We still have much of the queen's business to attend."

And that's exactly what we did. Somehow, the throne room moved on from its display of Raven Court patriotism and continued with more petitions. None were as exciting as what we'd heard from the Court of Stars, though.

The very long day concluded with a shopkeep asking the queen for a 12-month moratorium on tax duties so she could expand her tailoring business from Perth into the neighboring village of Sanc Red. Once the queen granted her this, she dismissed the nobles. Within minutes, the throne room was empty and quiet as it hadn't been since before sunrise.

I stood with the queen and stretched, wagging tail and rear rising while my front paws carried forward as far as they could. A yawn forced my jaws open wide for its escape.

Varella chuckled and ran her fingers under my chin.

"You did well today, my pet. Fierce and frightening as always you are at my side. My bargain continues to be fruitful. Are you ready to call it a day? Shall I summon your inner girl again?"

I nosed her arm, and the queen smiled.

Then she placed a hand over my head and called forth to the magic she kept within my wolfheart. It echoed within my core, responding to her will, reshaping me into the human girl that struck the bargain in the first place.

"Retreat, my wolf. Sierra Chelsi, I call you forth."

A familiar smoke rose from the stone floor, engulfing my entire body so the transformational magic could take place.

My instincts sank into an inner slumber to be called upon whenever the queen saw fit in the future.

***

I stood on two legs once more and stretched. The smoke around me thinned, vanishing as the queen removed her feathered cloak, wrapping me in it as she often did when I appeared naked after each transformation.

"Fun day at court, my queen?" I asked, yawning.

My stomach grumbled, and I felt a familiar light-headedness that came when assuming a human form again.

"You certainly ensured so, my little wolf. I believe I promised you dinner and some answers about Bliss. Shall we head to your room to get dressed for an evening meal?"

"I'd like that very much, mistress," I said, smiling.

Finally! I can have her all to myself, I thought.

My mistress ran her nails through my hair, which, as usual, left me frozen in a dizzied state while I absorbed every moment of her touch, head slumped to the right against her breasts.

"We'll go when you're ready," she taunted.

I couldn't budge, and she knew exactly why.

Maybe dinner wouldn't happen after all.

CHAPTER THREE

Was I pathetic enough to pretend I was too dizzy to walk up the stairs to the dining room just so I could lean heavily on my mistress? Yes. Did she take the hint and decide to carry me bridal style just to one-up me? Also yes. I'm ashamed to admit I'd really taken to my new job as the queen's pet over the last few months, absorbing every single ounce of her attention by any means necessary.

Okay, maybe I wasn't that ashamed. But she flaunted her attention and spoiled me rotten after a shitty 21 years. How else did she expect a brat to react except by making it her problem?

And it wasn't like she was unarmed in our game of "drive each other mad." Varella was the fucking Raven Queen. She had all the magic that comes with a dark throne of Faerie. She knew I was powerless against her domineering ways, and there was absolutely no armor I could equip to defend against her piercing and all-knowing gaze.

The way her violet eyes were capable of drowning me in a sea of surrender, the way her fingers could find any inch of my body to spread shivers, and the way her voice would slip into my subconscious, lulling me into whatever plans the eternal mind of an arcane monarch concocted rendered any fight I put up against her charms null and void.

But I liked that. Gods be damned, I liked it a lot. I was enthralled with the ways she owned every inch of my body, mind, and soul. The feelings I'd get when I knew just how deeply she held me left my body quivering in anticipation of whatever the fuck she wanted to do next, be it melting me in a puddle of cuddles or unleashing a surprisingly horny corner of my mind I'd not had much chance to explore before striking my bargain with the queen.

And that wasn't the only thing I wanted to explore. The fae carrying me to dinner was seven feet of muscled goddess I'd only had the pleasure of being metaphysically fucked by a few times since my arrival.

It turns out heavy is the head that wears that modest silver crown and sits on the corvid throne. If the CEO of a Fortune 500 company gets a puppy, she doesn't get to drop everything and spend all her time playing with the pet. She should. But this is a queendom that has stood for centuries. The court doesn't merely prop itself up while the queen is distracted, much as I wish that were the case.

A smile spread across the queen's face as she asked, "My pet? You seem so lost in thought. What occupies your mind?"

What was I supposed to do? Confess that fantasies of further domination had cornered my attention span once more? Never!

"I was just thinking about— what we're going to eat. You know, because I'm famished from the werewolf transformation."

Yeah, she totally bought that, I thought, surprised by

my quick lie.

"Oh, I think you're hungry, starving even. But not just for dinner, my little wolf," Varella said, before holding me up to whisper in my ear. "I think you're dying for dessert as well."

Heat rushed to my cheeks, and I found myself immediately disarmed in our game. But my metaphorical sword hadn't just fallen to the ground, she'd flicked it from my hand so hard that it flew into a stone wall 20 feet away. Just to remind me of our vast difference in ability.

I had no more words being so disarmed. So the queen chuckled and continued walking up the tower.

A few minutes later, we sat at an ornate round table that I'd sometimes fantasized about the queen taking me on. A silver cloth covered the table under our plates and black cloth napkins. Candles in the shape of baby crows were the only thing lighting our meal. They were enchanted so the wax didn't melt. I loved looking at the little corvids that appeared to be hopping around the table.

One of the kitchen staff brought in a plate filled with veal scallopini and a bowl of sliced plums. Steam skipped into the air and over to my nostrils, leaving me feeling like I was about to float over the table like in those old cartoons.

Carefully, I watched the queen pick up her silverware and dig in, always making sure my mistress took the first serving. Because she was worth it. The behavior was a small display of subservience, but I sometimes caught a little grin of acknowledgment when I waited a beat to bite my food.

I tore into that veal as though it was my last meal, and the tenderness of this cut paired with rosemary and thyme opened the gates wide enough for a little moan to escape my throat.

The kitchen staff had stayed around just long enough to receive that unintentional compliment before nodding his head and retreating to the meal prep area.

Goddamn, I eat better as a pet than I ever did in my mortal life, I thought, emptying half my plate in two minutes flat. What could I say? As a werewolf, I had little control when it came to appetite control. The beast wanted to eat and without any delay, none of that "savoring your food" shit. Tongue to belly was almost a race.

I'd just devoured a plum when the kitchen staff returned with a bottle of Pinot Noir and a pair of crystal glasses. He poured them half full and then retreated once more as I sipped from my cup.

"So, my pet, I'm sure you've been curious about my plans and why I've been so busy these last couple weeks," she said in between bites of pasta.

That's an understatement, I thought, taking another sip of my wine.

"Am I allowed to know what it is if even your talons don't know?" I asked.

The Raven Queen nodded and showed no reluctance whatsoever, which surprised me. What secrets do you share with your pet but not your knights?

"It's all about Bliss," the queen said, taking another bite of food. Outside near the balcony, a blue jay was making final calls for the evening before settling into its nest. I waited for the queen to tell me what Bliss would entail.

"I've been working on planning the biggest revel in Faery. Bliss is an event held once a century, and nobles from every court gather to celebrate," she said.

I cocked my head to the side a little.

"You've been planning a giant party?" I asked.

The queen chuffed, and I shrank back into my chair a little bit. Apparently, this was a stupid question to ask. But the queen didn't look upset. This was merely another concept she'd have to explain to a mortal who now called Faerie home.

"It's more than just a party, my pet. Bliss is a celebration centered around the Rosemund Comet, which bathes all of Faerie in unique magic for just a few hours. It's an intoxicating energy that fills every fae with the nourishment of eternity. The stone of cold fire refreshes our spirits so that we may carry on another century without the burden of time," she said.

Yup, that was a stupid question, I thought.

"My apologies, mistress. I didn't mean to downplay such a significant event. Obviously, this is more important than I could know," I said, finishing my meal, and placing my silverware on the plate to signal to the kitchen staff that I was done.

Taking a sip of her wine and licking her lips in approval, Varella waved her hand in a way that said "No harm, no foul."

"The celebration serving as bookends to Bliss is a revel to end all revels. You already know that we fae are creatures that carry an overt fondness for riddles, dancing, and games. We celebrate many things with drink and merriment, but also the Wild Hunt and a spirit of fervor given chase. But Bliss is something entirely more grandiose."

Nodding, I looked across the table at my mistress, taking in her lesson on the happenings of immortal creatures.

"So this meticulous planning on your part has all been to get Perth ready to host Bliss? Like the festival for the dryads?" I asked.

The queen finished eating and placed her silverware on top of her plate as well.

"Exactly. In one week, the Faerie courts will meet at Kilgara, the one sacred and neutral place in all of our lands. There, the kings and queens of every court will present their plans for the revel and decide which palace will host the celebration," she said.

All trace of flirtation and levity fled the queen's face as she went over her intent. I could feel a weight upon the room that didn't usually exist when we were together. And. . .was I imagining things, or did the queen's heart speed up a little just now?

She's nervous about this, I thought.

"And you intend to host Bliss?"

The queen nodded, finishing her wine.

"I do, my pet. Because when Bliss is complete, whichever land that hosted is permitted to ask a boon of any court in Faerie that attended the revel. And that land must grant the request, no matter what," she said.

"It's like a wish," I said.

"Of sorts."

After the plate and cutlery had been cleared away, we were treated to a large pile of lemon bars that crumbled perfectly in my mouth.

Another moan escaped as I reached for a second treat before I'd finished the one on my saucer.

"Mistress, will I travel with you to Kilgara?"

"Do you wish to go?" She asked.

I might have nodded faster than ever before, nearly causing my brain to rattle around in its thick noggin.

"I'd love to see the most sacred place in Faerie, and since it's neutral ground, then it'll be perfectly safe, right?"

The queen rubbed her chin lightly before staring out the window as the sun was dismissed in place of its pale sister.

"Nothing in Faerie is perfectly safe, my pet. Remember that. You have a posh life here, and I spoil you at my pleasure. But if you go out there, it'll be in the form of your beast. Just because we're meeting in neutral territory doesn't mean we can't be attacked en route," she said.

I slowly nodded, coming to understand what all that would entail. My wolf form for travel there and back? I guess that was only fair since my inner wolf didn't get nearly as much time on the outside as I did. And the queen would want me armed with fangs and claws to defend myself if some other court tried to prove itself.

I'd finished a third lemon bar by the time another question rose to mind.

"Do you have any more preparations to make in your plans before we leave for Kilgara?" I asked.

The queen thought for a moment and then shook her head.

"No, I'm pretty much finished. But we will make a short trip tomorrow for one final bit of business. After that, it's just a matter of waiting for the presentations and practicing my persuasion."

I watched golden light dance upon the crow candles before a grin broke out across my face. If her preparation was done, then. . ..

"Mistress, you could always practice your persuasion on me before the event. I'd love to help you in any way I could," I said, tapping a finger on the tablecloth.

Varella's smile matched my own as one of her legs found mine under the table, and she slipped off a shoe to rub her foot against my own. Gooseflesh dotted my arms and thighs as I stared into her eyes again.

"Oh, I already know I can persuade you to do anything, my pet. It's one of the things I take great pleasure in, ravishing you like no other. But as I suddenly find myself with a little more free time, I imagine we could rehearse my skills in the art of persuasion. And perhaps when I'm finished speaking, my silver tongue could find other things to practice," she said with a sultry stare that once more left me flushed, cheeks burning like you wouldn't believe.

She continued stroking my foot with hers for a moment as our legs flirted under the table to match our stares above the cloth.

Varella stopped when the kitchen staff came to remove our dessert. The lemon bars hadn't survived.

One last question popped into my head, and I raised an eyebrow.

"My queen. . .where exactly are we going tomorrow?"

Without missing a beat, she replied, "Why, to meet my brother, of course."

CHAPTER FOUR

We prepared to leave early the next morning to visit Varella's brother. My mistress possessed an unreadable expression about the trip. It was an otherworldly stare that she carried from room to room making sure we were set for the journey.

Imagine the world's greatest poker face. Then, add an otherworldly element because fae are so very far from mortal. Now layer on the power of a centuries-old queen. And that just might begin to explain how unreadable the queen truly was.

I'd witnessed her be terrifying, and I'd seen the queen flirtatious. It didn't seem like the energy radiating from her now was commonplace for her.

As we tarried in the tea room, I detected the approach of the second most powerful faerie in the Raven Court. She carried the scent of carnations and mint. Turning to face Lady Bon-Hwa, I bowed my head to show proper respect to the queen in command.

Today she wore an elegant silver gown, hair tied back with thin matching ribbons. Her brown eyes met mine when I raised my head.

"Your grace. . .are you heading out so soon?" Lady Bon-Hwa asked, tilting her head to the side.

"Yes, it can't be helped. I'm on the clock to finalize some important plans, and I need counsel from someone with a greater mind and eyes than mine," she said. "Will you take tea with the prince from the Court of Stars and hammer out a basic agreement to absorb fleeing refugees if his land should fall?"

Lady Bon-Hwa nodded, considering this.

"The Fist of Kairn is becoming a problem. Should we expect other nations to ask us for refugee shelter after being invaded?" the queen in command asked.

With a surprising sigh, the Raven Queen shrugged.

"We don't have the resources for that. And if we take too many in, it eventually opens us up to attack from the Fist of Kairn when the war explodes from its northern borders. That's why I need to get these plans finalized and ultimately sway over other rulers at our upcoming gathering," Varella said.

"I understand. I'll meet with the prince and negotiate a treaty for potential refugees that won't put our security in a bind," she said.

The queen cleared her throat, fussed with her hair for a moment, and then thanked Bon-Hwa for her help.

"If you'll excuse me, I'm going to check with Ceras so they know to expect an updated security policy soon. When I return, we'll leave, my pet," the queen said.

She departed and left me with the faerie who would sit the Corvid Throne today. When Varella was out of earshot, Bon-Hwa turned to me with a stare of contemplation.

"I haven't seen her this nervous in quite some time. It's a good time for her to visit the Word Sage," the queen in command said, walking over to the table.

Without thinking, I quickly moved to grab the kettle and poured the still-hot water into a cup that contained a wooden tea infuser. It was decorated with tiny carvings of feathers as so many things were in this palace. And I didn't even know how one would begin to design this many kitchen items with birds or feathers.

Does Faerie have its own version of Bed, Bath, and Beyond? I thought, putting the kettle back.

While I waited for the tea to steep, I kept my eyes locked on the cup, as if it would get up and run away should it remain ignored. Silence filled the room, and it didn't seem like my mistress would return anytime soon.

My shoulders slumped a little as I tried to loosen my upper back. I was tense because Varella was tense. All morning long I'd listened to her elevated heartbeat and smelled her sweating more than usual.

Only now that she'd left the room did I realize my fingers had been clenched at random points throughout the morning.

"Even when she's away, your thoughts lie with your owner, is that right, royal pet?" Bon-Hwa asked me, my ears twitching at the sound of her silvery voice. My mistress' tone was often smoky and danced around my ears with a lower timbre than other fae that spoke to me.

But Bon-Hwa's voice was more aetherial. She was a faerie who valued nuance in a way that even other word spinners would find disarming.

I motioned wordlessly toward trays of sugar and honey, but she merely shook her head. So, I slid the teacup and saucer closer to the queen in command.

She took the cup thoughtfully and sipped the amber liquid before slowly nodding. I watched steam drift over the handle when she placed the drink back on the saucer.

"It's good that the queen will see her brother today.

She needs him in more ways than one. This business with the northern war weighs heavily on her mind," Bon-Hwa said. I wasn't sure if she was talking to me or just reciting her thoughts. But eventually, she did look my way.

"This trip will be good for you as well, Sierra," she said, taking another sip of her tea.

"Me? How so, my lady?" I asked.

She looked me over with a strategic eye for a moment before answering.

"You're still learning about the many faces we wear in the land of Faerie. It's often difficult for mortals to know which face is the truest expression of ourselves. Or if each one we wear is an equal representation of the different pieces of an ageless mind," she said, tracing the edge of her porcelain cup with one of her nails, all of which were painted red.

I raised an eyebrow. How many faces had I seen of my mistress? It was a question I didn't ponder much because I figured she was genuine with me all the time. Perhaps that made me ignorant. Or maybe Lily's tender expressions of affection left me optimistic that I'd seen similar kindness from Varella, even if it was a different flavor.

"You think I'll witness a different side to my mistress today when we visit her brother, is that it?"

Bon-Hwa nodded without any accompanying grin.

"I can almost guarantee it. Vyzella brings out a different side of her. For you, I believe it'll be a treat," Bon-Hwa said.

Slowly nodding, I considered this. Varella had spoken little of her brother, leaving me to suspect they weren't all that close. But the queen in command was making it sound like they had an unshakable bond.

"What about you, my lady?" I asked, a strange curiosity

plaguing my mind.

"Me?" She asked, finishing her tea.

I scratched the back of my head and tried to figure out how to form my question. Because now that I was having an actual conversation with her, I found myself desiring to know more about the elusive fae before me. And she was elusive.

When she wasn't on the throne, so few people knew where Bon-Hwa went and what she did with her time. Or maybe I was the only one who didn't know. In the three months since I'd called Featherstone home, I'd maybe seen her six or seven times and spoken to her half as many.

But here we were. I suddenly realized curiosity wasn't only for cats. And what else would we do waiting for my mistress to return?

"Yes, my lady. You. You speak of our queen wearing multiple faces. So now I'm curious. How many faces do you wear?"

Her smile grew, and my heart skittered to a halt because I realized this had become a dangerous game in a matter of seconds. Had I grown too comfortable here in the palace to drop my guard? Or was I simply paranoid?

"I do wear different faces, royal pet. The number is not for you to know. But I will offer you this. . . .my true face. Because that is what I believe you seek. Your mortal heart longs for authentic expression in others. Our queen and her wing gave you those things willingly. But I am not your owner or your girlfriend. I won't give you my true face for free, little wolf. So what will you offer me for a glimpse?"

Bargains. That's what got me into this whole predicament in the first place. The Raven Queen had shown up when I was in a desperate spot and offered me a bargain. Now I was hers. Sure, I'd lucked out because she ended up being the best thing to ever happen to me. But other mortals were seldom as fortunate in their dealings with fae, finding their eyes turned to stone or their years cut in half.

What then would the queen in command ask of me?

I don't have the slightest clue what to offer you, I thought. And now that we've entered negotiations, I believe it'd be rude for me to suddenly retreat or call them off.

So, I decided to turn the table back toward the queen in command.

"What would you have of me to see your true face?" I asked.

To my surprise, Bon-Hwa's expression grew stern. Her smile faded, and I felt my heart sink with this change in her temperament.

"You need more training in wordcraft, royal pet. The first rule of bargaining with fae is never to let the one you want something from name their own price. It is the same as handing over your sword at the start of a duel," she said.

Shit, I thought. That seems like such an obvious lesson, too.

In my defense, I didn't exactly have anyone to teach me about the inner workings of fae here. I was pretty sheltered. Lately, my mistress has been busy, and my girlfriend was away on assignment.

"In exchange for seeing my true face, you will sit with me," Bon-Hwa suddenly announced, her frown lifting a little.

I sighed in relief. She'd decided to take it easy on me.

"Okay, deal. Thanks for giving me a break there and not asking for half my years or an eyeball," I said, going to sit in a chair opposite the queen in command.

"What are you doing?" she asked.

"I'm. . . . .going to sit with you? Like you asked," I said, frozen, unsure as to where I'd fucked up.

Her tone was stern again as she slid her teacup and saucer toward the center of the table. And I felt my chest tighten.

"You agreed to sit with me, little wolf. So come," she said.

And before I could ask what she meant, I watched the ribbons in her hair, those sleek, colorful strands of woven silk, extend and reach across the table. The queen in command didn't appear surprised by this in the least. She must have had at least four ribbons, and they wrapped around my thigh and torso. My ability to object took a backseat as Bon-Hwa's ribbons effortlessly lifted me above the table like I weighed as much as a doll.

They carried me back toward the powerful fae, and to my mortal apprehension, placed me gently in her lap.

"Excuse me?!" I stammered as her ribbons retreated to their original length.

"You assumed I meant for you to join me at the table. Another mistake, little wolf. Our queen is heavily invested in your well-being, and you have very little ability to defend yourself from traps and bargains. That makes you a liability. Because as much as she'd deny it, the Raven Queen's greatest weakness is now. . . .you," Bon-Hwa said.

I didn't try to get up, knowing she could just as easily ensnare me again. But my heart sure did take off like a jackhammer. The concrete of my inner foundation was being chipped away at a record pace.

And yet, the queen in command did not seem to regard our sudden decrease in distance with any flirtatious intent as my mistress would've. It seemed she did regard me as some doll or plaything, placing me on her lap as she might a blanket or a pillow.

"Pity. Talon Ceras has been training your body for the last two months but not your mind," the queen in command said, pulling my hair back behind my shoulders. I'd let it grow since arriving here in the Raven Court. Though it wasn't much past my shoulders, just enough for her fingers to push it back.

"May I get up now?" I almost squeaked.

"No. Because you agreed to my bargain believing I was taking it easy on you. We could sit here for a century if I wished. And you'd be powerless to rise because of our bargain. I am not your girlfriend or mistress. I'm not here to take it easy on you," she said.

I scoffed.

Play stupid games, win stupid prizes, I thought.

"So. . . .are we going to sit here for a century? I do think your legs will get sore long before then," I said, rolling my eyes.

She ignored my question and slid one hand around my waist, causing me to yipe. Still, I did not jump up as I wanted to. The other hand she reached across my torso and placed over my heart. I shivered. Though her touch was much warmer than that of Varella, there was no dalliance present.

I did my best to stop shivering like a girl at her first middle school slow dance.

"What are you doing?" I asked when my voice came back.

"I want to see the wolfheart that has our queen so ready to move Heaven and Earth for a pet. Now, sit, dog. It's the first trick you canines learn, the simplest."

Fuck you! I thought, scowling. I am not your dog to

command. I am Varella's bitch, and hers alone.

Of course, I didn't say this because the queen in command could easily rip my still-beating heart from my chest or change it into a water balloon for all I knew.

"Take a deep breath, royal pet. My glamour is about to find your wolfheart," Bon-Hwa said.

"How about you just let me tell you where it is? My wolfheart is tucked away in my chest. There, saved you some time," I said.

She shushed me. The queen in command actually shushed me.

Fucking hell, I thought, taking a deep breath.

When her glamour met my body, I shivered. It did not lull me into submission as Lily's did. The magic didn't subdue me with absolute power as Varella's did. No, Bon-Hwa's glamour ran all over my body, like she was looking for a weakness in my armor. It did not take her long to find whatever she was looking for, and when that weakness was located, her magic slipped inside without so much as a warning.

I gasped.

"Easy, pet. Steady. I'm not going to hurt you. I just want a peek," she said, and I steeled myself for this so-called peek.

Her glamour now felt like a viper that'd found a mouse's nest. The reptile slid quietly inside, crawling through tight spaces and pathways until the seeker found what it was looking for.

As her glamour wound its way down into my chest, it felt like slithering, finding every passageway imaginable. I almost felt scared to breathe, wondering what else I'd feel if my insides expanded or shrank while her magic was inside me.

I didn't have to ask when she found my wolfheart. Her

glamour made it blindingly obvious, coiling tight around the ball of magic in my chest. And at that moment, I understood that Bon-Hwa knew me.

She'd quite literally taken a look into my very core. Hell, the fae still was, eyes closed, breathing calmly as though she was just taking a stroll down the hallway.

I wasn't sure what to think. She wasn't hurting me, but I also felt like a body on a table with my insides on display for the coroner to see. And Bon-Hwa hovered over me, peeking inside, taking mental notes about the positioning of everything in the werewolf before her.

"Now I see," Bon-Hwa almost whispered.

Taking a breath and raising an eyebrow I asked her what she saw.

The viper around my wolfheart coiled tighter as if to absorb some heat and some strength. My inner wolf, stirred from slumber, growled, eyes revealing a simple message to the queen in command.

"I am not yours. Get out," she growled.

Bon-Hwa chuckled.

"You're a lovesick puppy with little wisdom to spare, Sierra Chelsi. But I finally see what the queen covets within your heart. It is a fierce loyalty. There's more to your dynamic with her than simply being a submissive wolf. You'd fight anyone for her. Because even if to all the rest of Faerie it appears she ensnared you with a complex bargain, the truth is, you're convinced with all of your heart that she rescued you. And you'd give her anything she asked for in return, even your very wolfheart," she said, glamour finally withdrawing from inside of me.

While I tried to shake the feeling of her little peek from my core, Bon-Hwa said nothing, considering what she'd seen.

"Are you satisfied with what you've found?" I finally

asked, wondering why I was still sitting in her lap.

"I'd say what I learned here today shows me you're even more naive than I anticipated. Viewing Varella's binding you to her as a mercy and a rescue is beyond mortal ignorance," she said, as I sighed.

But then Bon-Hwa's voice softened just a hair. The change was even less perceptible than when Barsilla did it.

"Though considering the harsh home you endured before coming here, I suppose it explains your outlook. And werewolves, though rare, can be powerful creatures, you more so armed with that large piece of magic her excellency implanted within your wolfheart. I see why she spoils you so. You're probably the one person in this court more dedicated and loyal to her than any other. Your physical and emotional subservience to your mistress is unlike anything I've ever seen. And with war spreading to the north, I believe that will be a notable asset to her majesty."

I placed my hands on Bon-Hwa's arm around my waist, knowing she was absolutely correct in her assessment. And I decided to play a card that was perhaps a little risky given how much of me she'd just seen.

"I've upheld my end of the bargain, my lady. Now you must show me your true face," I said, trying my best not to stammer or trip over my words.

She sneered, exhaling through her nose.

"True enough. I will show you my true face after you return from Featherbrooke. I'm quite eager to see how you'll handle meeting Vyzella," she said.

"What! But you said—"

"I said I'd show you my true face if you sat with me. Let this be a continuance of the lesson. If you want something timely, make that part of the bargain. By leaving that unsaid, you put yourself at my mercy," Bon-

Hwa chastised me.

Huffing, I heard Varella's voice suddenly appear from across the tea room. Aw shit. That wasn't good.

Looking down, I didn't fail to notice that I was still sitting in the queen in command's lap with her arms around me. I tried to stand but found my legs wouldn't move. They wouldn't even twitch.

"I didn't say our sitting time was over yet, royal pet," she said in a tone professors often used when they remind students the bell doesn't dismiss them, the teacher does. Fuck those professors, by the way. When you pay thousands of dollars for tuition, attendance is at-will and they can— that was a pissy distraction I didn't need to revisit.

Panicked, I tried to remove her arms, but they were steel, and I was suddenly as powerful as Kermit the Frog when I needed to be Miss Piggy.

"Oh my. What has happened in the mere minutes of my absence? My pet, have you truly left the queen's service? Where's that unflinching loyalty Bon-Hwa was just describing?"

I tried to speak, but the queen in command put her hand over my mouth.

"I'm afraid the royal pet has taken a liking to me, your grace. I shall therefore bargain with you for her binding," she said.

Trying to pull her hands from my mouth, sound muffled behind her fingers, I started to sweat. I could breathe through my nose just fine. But the need to tell my mistress I hadn't betrayed her was overloading my brain.

Yanking with all my might, I felt no give in Bon-Hwa's grip.

"Well. . .I suppose it can't be helped. You'll have to find a way to deal with Lily. They are romantically intertwined, you know?"

"Oh, that won't be a problem. How about I offer you. . . .45 sapphires for the little wolf?"

That seems suspiciously low, I thought, having not a single clue about fae economics. But surely I'd be worth at least a couple hundred of anything, right? She just said werewolves were rare and — focus, Sierra! I need to break free!

"How could I refuse such a generous offer?" the queen asked, placing a hand on her cheek to feign surprise.

I was shaking now, trying anything to break loose from my grip. That's when I noticed the queen and her second-in-command laughing. It was a teasing laugh, and heat suddenly flooded my cheeks.

Bon-Hwa stood and placed me on my feet, which were fully under my control again. And the powerful fae continued to chortle at my expense.

All I could do was drag myself over to Varella and place my head upon her breasts.

"That was mean," I muttered.

She leaned down and kissed the top of my head, gently. Then she stroked the back of my neck and, oh fuck, it was just too hard to stay upset with the queen who knew all the right buttons to push in exactly the right order.

Her marking on the side of my neck was icy from proximity, and I shivered once from chill, twice from pleasure.

"I'd never leave your service," I muttered, still carrying as much grumpiness as I could muster.

"I know, my pet. And we've gone through this before. Even if you wanted to, you couldn't. You're bound to me through the magic of — not just any fair folk bargain — but a dark queen of Faerie. It would take a great deal of power to sever you from me," she said.

Shrugging, I buried my face further into her breasts.

"And that's just fine with me," I said.

Behind me, I heard Bon-Hwa chuckle.

"My point remains. She is remarkably submissive," the queen in command said. But I ignored her. My mistress was here.

"But?" Varella prompted, staring at her.

"But. . .also remarkably loyal. I'll see to the Star Court prince, your grace. I wish you both a safe and enjoyable trip," the queen in command said, leaving.

The queen nodded at her and turned back to me.

"Time to go, my pet," she said.

"Are we flying to Featherbrooke?" I asked.

Varella simply shook her head and led me out of the tea room. We moved into a deeper part of the castle past the throne room where court was held and eventually came to a large bedroom door where two armored talons were stationed.

They stood at attention as we approached, and I noticed their eyes on me. Varella paid them no mind but opened the door and led me inside.

"Are we not going outside, your grace?" I asked.

"No need. Flying there would take a while. I'd much rather use that time to receive counsel from my brother," Varella said.

Looking around, I noticed we were in a fancy sort of mud room that connected the hallway to my mistress' bedroom.

There were no windows here, just a few pieces of furniture and painted black feather banners on the walls. Light drifted across the room from a single-burning torch of purple fire, casting deep shadows along corners and the ceiling several feet above us.

Against one wall next to the torch stood a large basin

full of silvery water. It was the size of several barrels and stood on four curved legs carved from brass.

Beneath our feet, a thin black carpet separated toes from stone flooring.

What really caught my eye, though, was a table against the wall opposite the basin. It was decorated with a rich violet cloth and covered in saucer-sized crystal discs, each containing moving images on a loop.

One showed a teen Varella with much smaller wings dueling a taller masculine-presenting faerie, each wielding black feathered blades. Another showed the Varella that stood beside me now, playing chess across from the same guy she'd been dueling. The final crystal saucer showed Varella as a little girl, diving into a pond and splashing water all over the individual pictured in every other image.

I giggled when I saw her splashing the older fae, their arms raised with a look of shock on their face.

"Your. . . .brother? Is that Vyzella?" I asked, realizing the queen had been patient enough to let me look at each moving image without rushing us along.

"The one and only, my pet. He's essentially the only living family I have left. Each of these crystal frames holds a treasured memory," she said, walking over and tracing her fingers between the images along the oak table.

And then she moved to the table's center where a little snowglobe sat with unlit candles on either side. The candles were purple, and their holders, large talons carved from dark wood.

Upon closer inspection, I saw the inside of the globe wasn't filled with snow. Rather, a log cabin surrounded by what appeared to be a bog and forest.

Walking up to the queen, I pointed at the globe, and she said, "Our destination, my pet. Wait here a moment."

Varella produced a single black feather and walked over

to the torch of purple fire. Lighting the edge of the feather, she then walked back over to the candles, holding the flame down to each wick.

They then burned with a smaller purple fire, oval light dancing left and right on top of each wick.

Once the candles were lit, tiny red runes formed across the base of the snow globe, adding their own light akin to a certain evil ring. And, ironically, the language written in these runes was some form of Elvish or some other language of Faerie.

The glass over the globe took on a more translucent and fluid shape as I watched it catch light from the candles and runes.

"What's going on?" I asked as Varella blew out her feather, grinding it within her hand until it was no longer visible.

"Time to go, my pet," she said, grabbing my hand and pulling me, against all expectations, into the globe as though it were a bubble.

My brain didn't have time to ponder whether I shrunk or the globe grew. I just felt like I was falling for the briefest moment, lost in the momentum of fae magic dancing senseless to no beat a mortal mind could comprehend.

And then. . . suddenly, I was standing. My feet were on solid earth. Though my eyes took a minute to collect any discarded vision from that abrupt transition. If Varella looked into my eyes at this very moment, I was sure she'd see slot machines spinning like in the Tom and Jerry cartoons.

When I could see straight (or see gay in my case), I noted that before us stood a rather humble log cabin. The timber was sawed well, and everything looked as though it was made by master crafters, the kind of gods people on HGTV would bow down and worship without question.

Black shutters lined each window, blocked by dark curtains on the inside. The door was a well-polished red complete with a brass handle with feathers molded into the side.

Shingles made from thin cuts of obsidian covered the roof, and a weathervane with a raven on top pointed north but swiveled with the wind.

The air here was considerably more humid and smelled of damp lumber and a bog. That's when I realized we were in a forested bog, though the cabin rested in a large clearing.

A clap of muffled thunder caused my head to whip around and see the forest and bog were caught in a massive storm. Lightning flashed and arced above the trees. Branches bent nearly to the ground from gale-force winds. And the storm filled the woods in all directions around us.

Only the clearing remained dry in a pocket of calm cloudy gray sky. It was as if some invisible force was holding the storm from entering the clearing.

"Uh, mistress? Is that storm moving toward us or away?"

"Neither, my pet. It's suspended in one place, as it has been for centuries. Keeps Featherbrooke hidden from outsiders. Nobody makes it through that storm," she said.

I marveled at whatever force of magic could suspend and sustain an entire storm before Varella stepped closer to the door.

"Well, my dear little werewolf, are you ready to meet my brother?"

CHAPTER FIVE

A couple scents hit me as we entered the cabin, printed pages and somewhere in this place . . . a cat. That didn't bother me too much. For a werewolf, I got along strangely well with felines. It was the damnedest thing. Cats would make friends with the biggest dogs like it was no big deal. In many cases, the cartoons got it wrong. We didn't make a big fuss about cats.

For lots of dogs, the bigger we got, the more chill we became. And I guess that included friendships with creatures of the feline variety. It was usually the little yappy shits that gave us a bad name in terms of behavior, with huskies being the biggest exception to that rule.

I don't know what was bred into those obnoxious assholes to make them the way they are, but most of the bigger breeds were fairly relaxed. Newfies? Couch potatoes. Great Danes? Easy peasy. St. Bernards? The best babysitters in the world. Werewolves? Unless we were actively hunting or threatened by something, most of us were strangely chill.

And cats seemed to respect that chill. Hell, they gravitated toward it for reasons unknown to me.

The inside of the cabin didn't match the outside. This was no rustic scene, but a sprawling two-story home filled with polished hardwood flooring and skylights to give this place plenty of natural light.

A bifurcated staircase with a purple carpet folded neatly over every step led up to a wide set of double doors on the left side and a hallway on the right. My mistress led me to the top of the left section, and I noted the double mahogany doors before us, decorated with painted feathers and storm clouds.

Varella walked up to the doors and knocked in a pattern I could only assume was something left over from when she was a little girl, developing a secret code to talk with her brother.

In fact, she seemed entirely different with each step we took up the staircase. Her walk morphed into a lighter stride, her heartbeat slowed to a more normal resting pace, and I might have even heard her humming a tune foreign to my ears.

She almost seems. . . giddy, I thought, as I heard a man's voice from behind the door call out.

"Come in," he said with an orotund voice.

My mistress gave me a look that said, "You're going to love meeting him," and I didn't doubt her one bit.

We walked into a library that would put the one in Beauty and the Beast to shame. This room was twice as big. Some Barnes and Noble locations didn't have this many books.

And the smell of pages was almost overwhelming. It was as though someone had found a way to bottle up the scent of a used bookstore and then filled a 500-gallon barrel of it in this very room.

Ornate wooden bookshelves all fitted together and perfectly aligned filled every bit of wall space in each direction I glanced. Book spines of all different sizes and colors were smoothly arranged on each shelf.

Expansive, yet narrow windows were placed between some bookshelves, bringing in plenty of light. But a large chandelier filled with dozens of lit candles provided its fair share of light for the room as well.

And seated near a running fireplace along the far wall in a red velvet chair was a man who looked remarkably like Varella. No doubt about it. These two were siblings alright. Some relatives you can look at and know.

Vyzella's hair was the same shade of black but curly. He didn't let it grow quite to his shoulders, and it was held back on the left side with a silver feather pin. Where my mistress was built like a brick wall beneath her armor, Vyzella appeared a little shorter than her (though still a foot taller than me) and lanky.

A small pair of rounded glasses made his mossy eyes appear a little larger than they were.

The keeper of Featherbrooke wore a dark pair of trousers and a cream button-down shirt with ruffled sleeves.

Unlike Varella, no cloak adorned his backside. But his feet were wrapped in what looked to be the comfiest pair of slippers I'd ever seen.

"Hello, dear sister," Vyzella said without looking up from the last page of a worn red book in his hands. I think the title said something like A Treatise on the Orclands Vol. III.

That sounds like exciting reading, I thought, sarcastically Wait! Volume III?!

"Give me just a moment, Var. I've just got—" Vyzella started before his sister finished the sentence.

"—One page left," she said softly, wearing a warmer smile than I'd ever expected from a wielder of the Dark

Wind.

Wait. . .did he just call my mistress Var? I thought. I've never heard anyone use a nickname for the Raven Queen.

We waited for a moment, watching Vyzella's eyes scanning left to right across the final words of his fascinating publication on diplomacy.

As he finished, Vyzella gently closed the cover with both hands, stood, and walked over to a bookshelf where an empty slot awaited. Sliding the book into place as though he knew without a doubt exactly where it went the whole time, the keeper of Featherbrooke finally turned to welcome us.

When he walked toward Varella, I took notice that his movements were slower than that of my mistress, as though he had all the time in the world. Everything was urgent for the Raven Queen. And I guess that came with the territory of being a monarch. But the Word Sage? He had no pressures bearing down on him, none that I could see.

"Hello, Vyz," my mistress almost whispered.

"It's wonderful to see you again," he said before the siblings embraced. A surprising tenderness glowed from their hug as the pair held onto each other for several seconds.

It was a little awkward to sit and wait, sure. But I wouldn't have interrupted their reunion for anything now that I saw it. The way Vyzella's arms held my mistress as though no storybook could ever be more important than his little sister, and the way the Raven Queen seemed to drop her defenses as though she trusted no one more in all of Faerie showed me these two should've met up much sooner.

When they finally parted, each wore a familiar smile as two ageless beings who could encounter one another again and again while treating each meeting as though it were fresh and new, as a comet might pass a planet so many times in its celestial journey, each visit a magic and ceaseless wonder.

My mistress finally motioned toward me and said, "Vyz, I'd like to introduce you to my pet, Sierra Chelsi. Sierra, this is my older brother and the keeper of Featherbrooke, also known as the Word Sage."

Vyzella walked over toward me and kneeled, which left me instantly stammering. This was highly unnecessary. But before I could motion for him to rise again, he held out his hand, flat and patient.

What else could I do? I placed my hand within his grasp, and he wrapped his fingers around mine.

"Sierra Chelsi, it's lovely to meet you. I've read so many great things about you in my sister's letters. My name is Vyzella Tremayne. Welcome to my library," he said, with a slight bow of his head.

And that's when I noticed his glamour stirring, a subtle enchantment that felt like wind gradually glowing storm clouds away when the rain is all finished. It danced up my arm and then down to my feet.

"May you always know you are welcome here, young wolf. And in times of need, may your feet find their way to Featherbrooke, a place of rest and solitude," he finished.

When he released my hand, his glamour lingered on my feet a while longer. While that feeling dissipated, I finally managed to choke out, "It's a pleasure, Vyzella. Thank you for welcoming me."

His smile carried a genuine warmth that got me thinking about Bon-Hwa's words

again. . .faces. Was this his truest self? The caring Word Smith and doting older brother?

"You've certainly done a lot to keep my sister happy," the keeper of Featherbrooke said.

My cheeks flushed as impure thoughts raced through my head. I'd done a few things to keep my mistress happy, but not nearly as much as she'd done to me.

I didn't have a response to that, so I just nodded slightly as Vyzella stood once more.

"So, dear sister. What brings you to Featherbrooke this day?"

My mistress held out both hands, and a bundled series of papers wrapped in purple ribbon appeared out of nowhere.

"It's about Bliss, brother. I want your words before I take my proposal to the other rulers of Faerie at the end of the week," she said.

A look of surprise overtook Vyzella, as though this was the first time he'd heard of such a proposal. Wow. My mistress really had been keeping this close to her chest. Barsilla didn't know. Ceras didn't know. Not even her older brother knew.

The Word Smith's eyes swept over the documents as though he longed to devour whatever had been penned on the cornflour-colored parchment. His mouth parted as he sighed. And I could've sworn Vyzella looked. . .hungry? Like I would if someone placed a box of chicken nuggets before me.

He seemed ready to devour these words but kept himself in check.

"That's a significant development," the brother said, closing his mouth again. Then he looked over my mistress with a soft glance and said, "You're really making a play for Bliss. I can't believe it. Every time I think you've peaked in your rule of the Raven Court, you surprise me again. I can't wait to read your proposal, and I'm proud of you for going after this. Father would be beside himself."

Holy shit! I thought. Varella looks like she might cry.

The monarch who'd ensnared me in a bargain months ago in the forests of northern Maine was gone, metaphorically speaking. Before me now stood a younger girl, thrilled and beside herself to receive such praise and a compliment from her brother.

Bon-Hwa was right. Seeing this face on our queen was. . .almost like a privilege. I felt like I'd been let in on a secret only a handful of people knew.

My mistress' violet eyes looked down at her bundled papers and then back up at the doting brother who clearly meant the world to her.

"Thank you, Vyz. That means a lot. I wish he was here to see it," she said, her voice distant, lost in some memory stored in the mind of an ageless being. When you lived for so long, loss became a different animal entirely. But carrying the memory of someone for centuries was a kind of immortality in and of itself. At least, that's what Peter S. Beagle had taught me as a child.

The cabin walls creaked outside as a new wind seemed to find the clearing. Was the storm shifting? No, Varella said it was stationary. Somehow. I needed to ask about that when the time came because I was beyond curious how one pinned a storm to an area.

"Well, let's get to work. I'm eager to see your latest wordcraft," Vyz said as Varella handed him the documents. He looked eager as they met his grasp, as though the pages were golden tickets to get into a candy factory.

Varella's now-empty hand patted the top of my head, and while I struggled not to affectionately beg for more attention, I heard the soft pit-pat of toe beans behind us. Tearing my attention away from my mistress' touch, I saw a large cat entering the library.

The feline looked like a Maine Coon and carried a smoky fur pattern of black, gray, and silver. Of course, this particular fuzzy cat was about twice the size of the Maine Coons I'd seen back home in — well — Maine.

He strode into the library as though no doorway was capable of keeping him from where he wanted to be. And that was the magic of cats, I suppose. No matter where they found themselves, felines always had a talent for owning the space they occupied.

And that was certainly the case for this cat that wandered over first to me, sniffing at my legs in that delicate bounce felines have when their nose is buffering with a scent. "Snoot snoot," I always used to say when I saw a cat smelling something back in the realm of mortals.

To my utter surprise, the cat then spoke.

"Well, that was fast. She's been in your home for, what, five minutes? And you've already enchanted her?" the cat said with a voice that managed to be simultaneously ornery and airy, like Sabrina's cat if he lived with the embodiment of a dark and stormy wind for centuries.

The cat sniffed at me some more, standing on his hind legs and placing his massive paws on my waist to steady himself as he smelled my torso.

"Stars above, Vyz. She's marked with magic from you, your sister, and your girlfriend," the cat said, finally lowering himself back down to the ground. "This puppy is aglow in glamour she can't even comprehend."

And without even a little introduction, the cat walked over toward my mistress, where she leaned down and picked him up, petting the top of his head.

"Why hello, Kit. I was beginning to wonder why you didn't greet us at the door," the Raven Queen said as I raised an eyebrow at the newcomer.

Kit tolerated my mistress for exactly 30 seconds before leaping back down to the floor in that way cats do when they've had enough of someone's affections.

"I had more pressing matters to attend to," he said, wandering over and rubbing against Vyzella's leg.

"Like. . .finishing your nap?" the older sibling asked while leaning down to pet his sole companion at Featherbrooke.

"Exactly," the feline said, stretching as Vyzella gave him all the affection one owes a cat upon entering a room.

I just stood there processing Kit's words. I already knew I was carrying glamour from my mistress. She'd placed a significant chunk of her magic within my wolfheart. But — who and how. No, I just needed to ask, even if it made me feel stupid.

"I'm sorry, can we revisit me carrying glamour I can't even comprehend? Other fae aside from her majesty have placed their magic upon me?" I asked.

Kit's tail flicked to the side as he stared upon my mistress.

"You didn't pick the little wolf for her intelligence, did you?" he asked. I let it go because there was no sense in getting upset at cats. They are born with everything but a sense of shame.

And they know it.

"Apologies. I should have been more clear instead of relying on your sense of perception. It's just a minor enchantment upon your feet so you can always find your way back to Featherbrooke whenever you need to. The storm will part for you as you enter the bog in the future, should you arrive in any other way besides the enchanted path my sister uses," he said.

I slowly nodded.

"Okay. . .that makes sense, I suppose. This certainly

seems like a safe place. But who exactly is your girlfriend, Vyzella?"

The older sibling merely grinned at that and then looked down at Kit. The cat turned to match Vyz's gaze with his own orange eyes and said, "Let me guess. You want me to entertain the wolf while you work on the proposal with Var?"

"It's like you're reading my mind, you beautiful storm cat," Vyzella said, winking.

"Well, I've protected your home for centuries. I'd be a failure of a feline if I didn't learn to anticipate your actions in that time," he said.

My mistress walked over and placed a kiss on my cheek.

"Behave, my pet," she said.

I raised an eyebrow and suddenly felt a new weight on my shoulder as Kit leapt up to perch upon me, licking a paw.

"Oh, don't worry. Your pet is dim-witted and stained with mortality, but the one thing she won't be at Featherbrooke is a problem," Kit said, rubbing his paw on the side of his face.

Opening my mouth, I thought better on whatever wit I could attempt to wield against Kit and locked my jaw once more. There was no point. I'd be a brat for my mistress, but here in the company of strangers? It wasn't worth my energy.

"There, you see?" Kit said, thumping his tail against the side of my head. "The little wolf and I will be just fine. Now c'mon, Sierra. Let's leave the Word Sage and Raven Queen to draft the next Treatise on the Orclands."

I shrugged and turned to leave as Kit directed me out of the library and across the second-floor landing into that hallway at the other end of the stairwell.

"So. . .Vyzella called you a storm cat? What exactly. . .is that?" I asked, struggling to make conversation with the feline perched on my shoulder.

"Simple. I am a cat, and I make storms. For centuries, I have continued the bog-wide gale that keeps Featherbrooke protected and hidden via lightning bolts, furious gusts, and thunder loud enough to split your eardrums," he said, proud of himself in the way that all cats are. I'd never met a feline that didn't know how to be self-honored.

I cast a smile at Kit and found myself rather enamored with his ability to shield an entire home such as this in a nonstop cyclone. That was amazing.

"Wow, Kit. You've been sustaining a centuries-long thunderstorm that tears all who enter to shreds with just your glamour? That's kind of badass," I said.

The storm cat rubbed his cheek lightly against mine and said, "Sierra, my dear, I am, as you mortals put it, badass. And I think you and I are going to get along just fine. For a dog, you don't seem to carry quite as much insufferability as some of the other more abhorrent breeds."

I scratched the fae feline's chin as he purred and suddenly found myself a bit more enamored with Kit. Was this his glamour at work? Or was this just the ancient way of cats to capture the affection of all who gazed upon them?

"Oh, you mean huskies? Fuck those guys," I said as we entered a dining room.

Kit just laughed and said, "Yes indeed. Fuck them and the prick who first bred them. Wolves were perfectly fine creatures before mortals got to work on the abysmal process they called domestication. Thank the gods they never succeeded in doing that with cats."

CHAPTER SIX

Time rolled by with Kit. He guided me over to the kitchen on the other side of Featherbrooke. We sat at a polished wooden bar, small lit lanterns hanging from chains above us. For normal folks, this would be a little dark even for a dive, but for a storm cat and werewolf, it might as well have been a well-lit room.

Smells of wine and lavender filled this part of the kitchen, and when I looked around, I noticed potted flowers near a narrow rectangular window running behind us.

That would explain the lavender, I thought, inhaling again.

Like the library, it felt like this part of the manner was designed to feel secluded from the rest of the home, its own little nest tucked away in a space just for Kit, Vyz, and whomever they deemed worthy of entry.

Kit motioned over to a long shelf at eye level bolted to the wall. The wood matched that of the bar. Bottles of booze, but mostly wine, in colored glass, decorated most of the shelf. The whisky burned my nostrils when I got close, and I sneezed.

"No, no, young wolf. That's just for Vyz whenever the mood strikes him. I think he's drank from that bottle four times in the last 40 years. Grab the Torrington 275 bottle. One of my favorite years," Kit said, before lifting his paw toward a green bottle after noticing I was lost.

"Let me guess, almost as old as you are," I chuckled, expecting Kit to understand my Bilbo joke.

Of course, he did not. His eyes stared blankly at me as I grinned.

"Oh, goodness, no. I'm easily 300 years older than this wine we're about to drink. I just think the year it was made was particularly fun. I was in the Sunset Court at the time, and the king there gave me free rein to do as I pleased. The mischief I committed to for decades there was legendary. There are fae still furious with me for some of my hijinks," Kit said, motioning for me to grab some wine glasses.

Below the alcohol shelf, a rack of upside-down wine glasses hung, waiting to be used. They were so clean that even dish detergent commercials would be jealous. Whatever Vyz did to keep them that way was working well.

I grabbed a glass and also noticed a separate rack of metal saucers for, presumably, the storm cat. Hard to drink from a wine glass with paws. Maybe I should let my werewolf out to even the challenge.

As if I even knew how to do that on my own, I thought, grabbing one of Kit's bowls.

A searing heat raced through my fingertips as though I'd placed them on the coil burner of an oven on its highest setting. You know, the one where the entire coil is a dull orange.

"Motherfucker," I hissed, immediately dropping the bowl and licking my fingers that were still smoking. It wasn't much smoke, but to me, it might as well have been a forest fire's worth as the smell of charred flesh took hold of my nostrils.

Then came the throbbing when the smoke finally cleared. I could feel each beat of my heart in the scalding fingers.

"Holy shit! I'm so sorry, Sierra. I didn't even take into account my bowls were made of—" I interrupted the feline.

"Silver?"

It's difficult for a cat to look ashamed. You see videos and pictures of dogs with their ears drooping and tails tucked under when their owner points at a shredded couch or overturned garbage can. But cats? No shame.

And yet, Kit sounded genuinely sorry, a bit of sympathy filled the edges of his sunset-colored eyes.

"We've never had a werewolf visit here before. I'm sorry about that," Kit said, hopping off the bar, picking up the bowl with his teeth, and returning to his previous seat.

My fingers hurt worse when I bent them, so I poured our wine with the other hand after Kit removed the cork with his teeth.

I filled the feline's bowl first while shaking my hand. My digits weren't smoking anymore, but they were covered in a thin layer of black scorch marks on my fingertips.

Been a while since I've touched silver, I thought.

We're pretty hardy creatures with a speedy recovery time compared to vanilla humans. But silver fucks us up as iron does for fae. My fingertips would probably be scorched for the rest of the week.

I walked over to Vyz's sink, which was filled with copper pipes and probably pulled from a well. Turning a knob, I let cold water run over my singed fingers for a minute before drying them on a nearby towel.

When I returned, Kit started drinking wine from his bowl. I took a sip and found it to be pretty dry, more so than I was used to at Featherstone. I shouldn't have been surprised to find Vyz and his sister having different palettes.

"So, you've been in Var's service for about three months now, I hear. But I still don't know how you ended up there," Kit said.

My mind went back to that fateful day in the forests of northern Maine. A desperate werewolf fleeing the consequences of her actions. Varella appeared out of shadow and offered me a bargain I found myself powerless to refuse.

"I'd just murdered my abusive father and was on the run from law enforcement. They were hot on my trail as I fled through the woods of northern Maine. That's. . .uh, part of the United States in the human world," I said.

Kit rolled his eyes and waved my geographical concerns away with his paw.

"Yes, yes. I know Maine. I've been there a few times on my trips into the mortal world. That's where the Scary Man lives."

I raised an eyebrow.

"You know, the mortal that writes terrifying stories. Vyz has a few in the library. This mortal's ideas are wild enough to give nightmares to even some fae. His stories carry value here in Faerie because of how dark and powerful they are," Kit said.

My brain was short-circuiting because I couldn't for the life of me figure out who Kit was describing.

"How can you not know this? His words are famous," Kit said, before changing into a more dramatic voice.

"The man in black fled across the desert, and the gunslinger followed."

Then it clicked.

"Oh! Yes, he's the most famous Mainer. I'm surprised you've heard his stories but not those of Tolkien," I said.

"What are you talking about? I've heard all of Tolkien's works. Why would you assume me to be ignorant of Middle Earth's creator?"

I sat there dumbfounded. Maybe Kit just hadn't seen the movies. That was probably more likely.

"Um— never mind. Anyway, my mistress offered me sanctuary in the Raven Court if I became her pet. And. . . I don't know. The whole thing is kind of a blur. The sheriff was closing in, and she just kept scratching my head with those long nails of hers. I'd have given her anything," I said, staring off into space and remembering the feel of her touch against me. It brought shivers to my shoulders.

Kit scoffed.

"You wolves are all the same, you know that? It's all, 'Oh! I'm so fierce, with my massive jaws and razor claws.' But you're practically puppies the moment someone scratches you behind the ears. You'd never see a feline lower themselves to such a humiliating level," he said, lapping more wine from his bowl.

I fought the urge to roll my eyes, biting my tongue and grinning.

"Yes, well, we can't all be born with the legendary resistance of cats," I said, taking another sip of wine.

The buzz was already building, and I sighed, relaxed. This place just felt safe. I didn't expect Kit or Vyz to lay a finger on me. We were sheltered by an eternal thunderstorm, let alone the fact that nobody knew where we were.

Was this how my mistress felt? Carefree? Able to lay down her burdens if only for a few hours while visiting Featherbrooke and the halls of her older brother? No wonder today had brought a different face out of her.

Of course, she wasn't here at the moment. Kit was, and I wanted to know more about him.

"Kit, how did you come to be in the service of Vyzella?"

Somehow the feline looked as though he expected this question. Perhaps my mind just wasn't that creative, only capable of copying his questions.

The storm cat motioned for me to fill his bowl deeper, even though it wasn't empty yet. But I did as he asked without hesitation. For what mortal would be foolish enough to deny a cat his heart's desire? They may never give anyone a straight answer, and sure, their pride knew no limits. But it was a fool's errand to resist their wishes. Even if it were physically possible to say "no," you'd pay dearly later. Everyone boasts of the memory of elephants, but the true masters of memory are feline minds, so long as the task at hand is vengeance, the pettier the better.

So, I pulled the cork free, hissing at the pain in my fingers again, and poured more wine into that silver saucer of his.

He purred in apparent happiness and lapped up more.

I wonder if Vyz lets him drink this much when it's just the two of them? I thought before correcting myself. Silly me. Nobody lets cats do anything. Their will simply is. And people in their vicinity have to quickly decide whether they're assistants or obstacles.

"You see, young wolf. And you are young by comparison to most fae, you see. It's not an insult, but a statement of youth in the face of ageless beings. And that's really how my story with the Word Sage begins," Kit said in between more drinks.

Each lap seemed to loosen his tongue just a little more, not that it needed much easing to begin with.

"The thing you must understand about immortality is it can become a burden after a while. Because the next while is all there is. The first two centuries are the best parts of your life. You taste everything you want and more. The third century is fine. But the fourth and fifth? Colors start to fade, and vibrancy is a drug you crave all the more."

As Kit spoke, a renewed weight poked at the edges of his eyes where sympathy snuck in earlier as I burned my fingers. His fur sank a little, and the whiskers that normally danced around his mouth appeared frail and thin.

"Let's just say I've been around for a long time, young wolf. And at one point, I was prepared to cross the Silver Bridge. You see. . . unless you possess a desire to shape the world around each footstep, or a drive to undrestand the mysteries of this path we call life, eventually the days become a weight. And some fae wish to cease carrying it upon their weary shoulders," Kit said, pausing to drink.

I almost raised my hand, as though I was listening to a college lecture from a learned professor of philosophy.

"Hey, Kit? What's the Silver Bridge?" I asked.

His tail twitched back and forth as the cat calculated the best way to explain how immortality comes to an end sans violence.

"It's a crossing into Death that faeries may choose when the years grow too many and the pleasures grow too few. That path leads us to the Witherlands, where we wait peacefully for a time while ageless minds and bodies are slowly dissolved into ash, their magic returned to the great ether and psyche put to rest. At one point, I was about to cross. Had a single paw already on the path," Kit said, motioning for yet more wine.

I granted him this, too immersed in the lesson on immortality to do otherwise.

"Vyz stopped me, asked if I'd remain with him until such a time came that we both would cross the Silver Bridge together, as the Raven King did with own storm cat companion," Kit said.

His answer had only created more questions for me, and I sputtered trying to get them all out at once. I don't think the Faerie wine was helping.

"Raven King? Is that Vyz's father?" I asked. "What did the Word Sage offer you in persuasion of facing more centuries together? How did he dissipate your weariness of the ages?"

Kit chuckled as his tail swished back and forth. I assume that to the feline I was as a five-year-old being read a story before the fireplace in preparation for bed. But the tale was too exciting, and reading it backfired because now I was more energized than ever, too curious for sleep to even knock on my door.

"Yes, that Raven King, the father of both your mistress and my master. When the crown grew too heavy upon his head, and many years were behind him, the king chose that crossing. Var was just a little girl at that point, so Vyz took her in and raised her here. As for what the Word Sage offered me? Stories. As many as my ears would hear. As often as I want, he reads me stories from his libraries," Kit said, batting at the side of his bowl with a loose paw.

I raised an eyebrow.

Libraries? Is there another grand library somewhere in Featherbrooke I don't know about? I thought, trying to imagine where it would be.

Surely all the thousands of books packed into the

library where we met Vyzella were enough to keep one fae's eyes occupied for all the days of their life. It was more than any mortal could read, even with two or three lifetimes. I couldn't imagine a second.

But another greater curiosity took hold as I cocked my head to the side.

"Wait— he reads you stories? I mean no offense, but. . .were you never taught to read?" I asked, finishing my wine and deciding against a second glass.

The room was already a little blurry at the edges of my eyes as I ran my fingers over the smooth bar to ground myself.

"Of course I know how to read, you silly wolf. I can read 52 languages, both mortal and ageless. That's not the point. He is the Word Sage. What greater gift could he possibly bestow than his sentences and soliloquies? When he tells me stories from the countless tales he's read, I have his full attention and whatever world of words he's building for as long as I desire. It is a new way of seeing Faerie and even your homeland, through his eyes. That is all I desire with the years I have left here at Featherbrooke. That. . .and wine, of course," he said, as I emptied the last of the bottle into his bowl.

Kit grew more talkative but never slurred his words as I nearly did when I spoke. And he'd swallowed four times the liquor I'd managed to stomach.

Next time I'm challenged to a drinking contest, I'm bringing a saucer and summoning my new friend here, I thought, remembering my inexplicable losses to Barsilla over the last few weeks.

We sat in silence for a moment as I let everything the feline had revealed sink into my mind. At some point, I realized darkness had fallen outside and wondered just how long we'd been talking.

Kit told me a few more stories, and I relayed some of my own. I was beginning to really like this cat when he suddenly grew more serious than I could imagine the feline being at any given moment. His sunset eyes locked with my own red irises as he spoke.

"That is our role as pets, you understand," he said.

"Our. . .role?" I asked, feeling a little more hydrated after downing a glass of water from the sink.

His tail thumped to the bar and did not move again until Kit had finished speaking. No licking paws or purring here, just relaying our mission, the sacred duty.

"We are their protection, Sierra Chelsi. Whether their physical or emotional safety is at risk through the long years, it's our sacred duty to be there beside them. The burdens of your mistress are many, but I see in you an unwavering dedication to her through it all," the storm cat said.

And I felt it stirring within me at that moment, the dedication he spoke of. It was warmth and pride in my choices to follow the Raven Queen — no — to give myself over to her entirely and in perpetuity. Everything surrendered, nothing held back, all for the sake of her safety, her happiness. She was worth it. I'd make the bargain again and again with her.

"You must also realize, young wolf, that although you might have merely imagined your service to last for a lifetime, if she so desires, Var could carry you into eternity with her. I smell her on you, the scent of night wind and blackberries. I smell her inside of you, Sierra, the tight ball of magic Var planted within your very core, ensuring you'd never be without her essence. And that energy has changed you in ways you aren't even aware of yet," Kit said.

Was he saying what I thought he was saying?

"Do you mean to say Varella has made me like. . .all of you?"

"This is what makes your total surrender to the Raven Queen so amusing. You hand yourself to her on a golden platter, let her tinker with your very being, and act surprised when the truth of change comes to light. Yes, Sierra, the queen has stripped you of your years. You serve her until she dismisses you, or Death claims you, tomorrow, a year from now, a century from now, a millennium from now. You are hers through the ages. That is what you agreed to as her pet," Kit said.

None of this made me nervous, per se. It's difficult to wrap your brain around being told you'll potentially live forever. Her magic ensured I'd accompany the Raven Queen for as long as she deemed necessary. That didn't bother me. I was just left more curious than anything. What did it mean for a werewolf to walk beside her mistress for an age? How could I even begin to understand that?

Stifling a sigh, I realized the queen-in-command was correct. I needed more wisdom if I was to understand this world. Faerie was a place that defied the mortal mind in so many countless ways. And I was part of it now, courtesy of the queen whose magic sat at the center of my being.

I heard footsteps entering the kitchen and turned to see the Word Sage wander in. His steps carried no urgency, and he looked tired, eyes drooping a little as he selected a different bottle of wine and poured himself a glass.

"Well now, Kit. Have you've taken it upon yourself to educate our guest in the ways of Faerie in my absence?" he asked, taking his first sip and nodding in approval.

I was just now realizing how much Vyz's voice sounded like that of Christian Bale, only much airier.

"The young wolf has been amusing, master. But I find myself emptied of words and full of liquor. If it's all the same to you, I'll depart now and join Var in slumber," he said, hopping off the bar.

I stood at once, immediately wishing I hadn't as the room spun a little. It was settled only as long as I was.

Steadying myself on the bar, I looked to our host and asked, "Where is my mistress?"

He gave me a gentle smile and motioned that I should once again follow the storm cat. Doing just that, I eventually found myself in a bedroom that I instantly recognized as Varella's. Tapestries and paintings of corvids hung from the wall. Her bed, barely large enough to contain all seven feet of her, was covered in a black quilt that she'd fallen asleep on.

Next to the bed sat a little table with a dimming lantern and several scattered parchments I recognized from earlier. This was the proposal they'd worked so hard on, and it was covered in scribblings and markings that likely came at the behest of the Word Sage.

Among the papers sat a small snow globe, though this one was filled with a lake and a familiar castle, our home.

I recognized Featherstone and marveled at the simplicity of how Varella could bounce between here and there.

The Raven Queen did not stir as Kit hopped up onto the bed and snuggled next to her tummy. I walked over, listening to her steady breathing.

I marveled at how disarmed the queen appeared, as though she'd truly cast aside her armor and shield so long as she found herself within the confines of Featherbrooke.

An aloofness possessed her here that she couldn't equip anywhere else in Faerie, because this was where she'd been a little girl, spending years growing up in the safety and happiness of her brother's home.

She even snored a little, something I never expected to hear from the queen.

Out like a fucking light, I thought, finding a folded cream-colored crocheted afghan on the bed frame.

I covered my mistress with it and kissed her lightly on the forehead, wishing nothing more than a bountiful rest for her majesty after many weeks of hard work.

"You finished the proposal for Bliss, my queen. Now I bid you rest, and sleep deeply, for you are safe. I am your pet and will forever watch over you," I swore silently, stroking her obsidian hair for a moment before turning to see Vyz in the doorframe.

He motioned for me to follow when I was finished saying goodnight. And when I hesitated to leave my sleeping queen, Kit spoke from under the blanket.

"I am here. As I protect your mistress, go accompany my master."

Nodding, I left her to the dreams of whatever queens imagined in their slumber.

CHAPTER SEVEN

"You truly are dedicated to my sister. It's impressive to see she's found someone who would follow her anywhere," the Word Sage said as we reentered the library. "The way you simply had to lay eyes on her instead of taking my word for it that she was safely asleep. That's quite a bond you've formed with her in three months."

He had no clue how right he was. And in the pit of my stomach, I did need to see her safe and sound. Vyz had been nothing but kind to me since arriving. That didn't stop me from being the queen's pet, though. And a pet watches over her mistress.

"I'm sorry. I didn't mean to imply I had no trust in you. You talk about needing to lay eyes on the queen, but to be honest, I don't know what you've done with her," I said, laughing a little nervously. I fidgeted with one of my nails, running my thumb over the back of it.

The words of our queen-in-command came back to me.

"Vyzella brings out a different side of her. For you, I believe it'll be a treat," she said.

And it did feel like a treat. . . seeing this relaxed side to my mistress that she lacked everywhere else. Inside this place, she felt comfortable enough to set her feathered armor aside and be vulnerable.

That's a dangerous word in Faerie, I thought.

The Word Sage looked thoughtful, but I was coming to recognize that was a default expression for Vyz. He had resting wise face.

"I assure you, I did nothing with her. . . except raise her of course. Featherbrooke was her home as a girl. Father was too busy ruling to take much interest in her life. Seemed he'd spent all his parental energy just getting me to where I wouldn't die if left alone. I didn't want that for her, for someone fated to wear the Corvid Crown," he said.

His gaze suggested the Word Sage was thinking back to those days, when a young Varella ran through the cabin, yelling and laughing as she bounded after Kit, likely making him question why he didn't just walk the Silver Bridge.

That picture made me happy, even if it was just part of my imagination. I'd seen my mistress on the battlefield. I watched as she cut down invaders from the Yellow Court, not a moment of hesitation as she struck them down. Hell, I was right there beside her, inner wolf spilling blood to keep her safe.

And it wasn't like I disliked that version of my mistress. But as Bon-Hwa said. . . that was one of her faces. It was the face of a deadly queen, wielder of the Dark Wind.

Here, though, Varella had been a mere girl, even if it was centuries ago. And she got to be that person again each time she came here. I found myself adding it to the list of things I'd protect for her. Featherbrooke was too important to otherwise ignore.

"So, Sierra. I was thinking that I'd like to give you a present, if you'd accept a gift from a total stranger, of course," Vyz said.

He wore a gentle smile, and for a moment, I found myself wishing he had been my older brother. Living alone in that fucked-up house with an abusive father was beyond lonely.

And if Vyz had been there, he might have protected me from that asshole, sprung me loose, and whisked me away to a cabin in the woods where he read me stories and let me play with his cat.

"A gift?" I asked, cocking my head to the left.

"Is that okay?" he asked. "I don't want to pressure you."

I nodded, finding myself trusting the man before me. If my mistress could lower her armor here and set it against the wall, I surely could as well.

The Word Sage walked over to a nondescript door in the wall I hadn't noticed. It was wedged between two massive bookshelves that swallowed up your vision when you looked in that direction.

Following, I noted the door was built into an exterior wall of the cabin. Outside in the distance, I heard a low rumble of thunder once more. Trying to make sense of this, I made a mental layout of what I'd seen of the building from the outside.

The wall I followed Vyz too should face the western bog.

But when the elder fae placed his fingers on the doorknob and twisted it, a rush of cold air washed over the library, blowing my brown hair back.

If I thought the library smelled of printed pages, then this gust of wind carried that scent 1,000 times over. Maybe a million times over.

It was the difference between smelling one cob of corn and an entire ripe field of the stuff, just ready to be harvested.

Beyond the door, I witnessed books as numerous as stars in the night sky above Featherstone. It was a number beyond counting, and ever more did it appear to grow.

Vyz and I walked into this place that I didn't have the words to name. Bookshelves stacked on top of each other beyond my vision, stretching up and over into a distance greater than my mind could comprehend. In truth, it was dizzying, just being here.

But the Word Sage inhaled deeply and instantly seemed at home. The air around us was so quiet that a tomb seemed like a rock concert by comparison. Sound was a negative value here. Or was that an imaginary number? I always had trouble with normal math, so of course the imaginary stuff was beyond me.

I suppose that made sense for fae, though. Imaginary is what most mortals assign to their description. And this was certainly a place where mortals did not tread.

"Where are we?" I asked, the sound of my voice vanishing the moment I'd spoken, as if the noise didn't wish to tarry a moment longer than necessary to reach the Word Sage's ears.

"In the Cosmic Library. This is a chamber with few doors and every book written after the mortal year 1455. They appear here on shelves that carry every tome you could imagine and more," Vyz said, sweeping his arms around the millions of books. It was the first grand gesture I'd seen him perform.

Now that I realized it, what exactly were we walking on?

Looking down, it appeared our feet hovered over nothing, a swirling void of pale greens and purples, glistening stars kept at some impossible distance. It made up the floor and the ceiling, as well as all the cracks and spaces between each bookshelf.

"Is this. . . really every book since. . . whatever that year was that you mentioned?"

The dizzying prospect of such a thing existing all around me threatened to overwhelm my mind. Certainly, there had to be limits to what the average human was capable of thinking.

Vyz rubbed his chin and thought for a moment.

"Give me the name of a book, Sierra," he said.

And — fantastic — I loved being put on the spot. I knew everything until the moment someone asked me a specific question. Where would you like to eat, Sierra? My brain struggled to name even one restaurant, let alone specific food.

My mind was randomly taken back to the easiest point in my life that I remembered. . . and coincidentally the one time I was happy before making my home in Faerie. Before bed at night, my mother used to read me the "Little Bear" books. She'd inherited a few of them from her mother, who read the stories to her before bed each night.

The pages were worn, and maybe I folded one or two. I might have even drawn on the back cover. But she never scolded me for it. Before she died, I always expected to inherit them as she had. But my father stole me away to Maine before I had the chance to pack them.

"Sierra? What are you thinking?" Vyz asked.

"Little Bear," I muttered. "It's from the 1950s, I think."

The Word Sage nodded and spoke aloud to the bookshelves as though they were living creatures awaiting his command.

"Please bring me Little Bear by the mortal novelist Else Holmelund Minarik," the fae said with an air of authority.

Within seconds, the bookshelves groaned and croaked as if the wood they were born from had been chopped, carved, and sanded hundreds of years ago. And every moment of age was made known to us by the noises every rack of books made shifting around. Some shelves grew larger, and others shrank.

Three or four bookshelves folded in on themselves only to be replaced by ones of different colors. And the rustling of pages! Thousands of them, a storm of change and alteration. This was alchemy of the printed word.

Seeing bound volumes vanish into thin air, only for that emptiness to be filled by renewed titles entirely.

When everything finally settled, I sneezed on the dust, and Vyz said, "Gesundheit" but unironically.

Varella's brother walked over to the shelf closest to him, and his finger traced over a few different titles that appeared to be in pristine condition.

"Ah, here we are. Little Bear, Father Bear Comes Home, Little Bear's Friend, Little Bear's Visit, A Kiss for Little Bear, and Little Bear and the Marco Polo," he said, pulling a copy of each book from the shelf.

And those weren't the only books around us. The shelf to my left was filled with nature guides on bears and what to do if someone encountered them on a hike. The shelf behind me was populated by crime novels with the word "bear" in the title. On a row to my right, books on stocks were crammed together, all written on the subject of bear markets.

Gingerly, I accepted the stack of literature from Varella's brother. Their weight grounded me in a room full of countless stories.

"Vyzella. . . I can't take these from your library. These are all first editions and must be worth a fortune," I said, rubbing my fingers lightly over their collective hardcover spines.

The Word Sage chuckled to himself.

"I assure you, Sierra, you can take them. They are my gift to you. Their value was never in a price of dollars and cents to me. I've never cared how much a mortal would be willing to pay for the rarest tomes in this vast collection. Instead, what I treasure are the words between each cover. Observe," he said. "Please bring me all the books by the mortal author Stephen King."

With another rush and rapid shifting of shelf placement, the bear books disappeared. And before my eyes, I saw every work by my home state's most famous celebrity.

"Holy shit. Cujo, Cycle of the Werewolf, Dead Zone, Firestarter, it's all here," I said, eyes widening as I looked around me.

Vyz scanned the tomes until he found a first edition of "Carrie," revealing to me the book was autographed.

"This would fetch a good price in any bookstore from your mortal world. This is one of the first copies published back from the year 1974 in your realm. But I don't care for any currency or price a human would put on this," he said.

I stood in silence listening as he explained.

"The true worth of this piece of literature comes in the form of commentary on the subservience of young

American girls placed under the burden of a mortal religion and what happens when one of them finally does something about it," he said, putting the title back on its shelf.

Clearing my throat, I said, "Yeah, Piper Laurie was pretty terrifying in that one."

I expected to be chastised for mentioning the movie in place of the novel, but to my surprise, Vyz chortled.

"Personally, I found Sissy Spacek to be the most horrifying part of that motion picture," he said.

No, I wasn't going to be shamed, certainly not by the kind brother standing before me. He didn't seem to mind that I hadn't read the book. He met me where I stood, in the cinematic adaptation. This only endeared him all the more to me.

"May I ask. . . why Little Bear?"

Thoughts returned to my bedtime stories as I looked down at the well-preserved books in my grasp. I held them up to my chest, my arms in the shape of an X, as though I could get them a little closer to my heart.

"Before she passed. . . my mother used to read these to me each night as I sat in my bed. She even sewed me a Little Bear pillow that I slept on. I guess, I just wanted to see that piece of my childhood again. Given my shitty life prior to coming here, I used to cry sometimes that my mother's books were lost to me. And now, thanks to your kindness, I have them back," I said, a single tear falling onto my wrist.

Looking at the spines again, I noticed an unfamiliar title.

"I don't think I've ever heard of the Marco Polo one," I said.

"Ah, yes. Ms. Holmelund Minarik published it in 2010, a little before she died, 42 years after the previous title. I read that one to Kit a few months ago. You'll never guess who his favorite character is."

Giggling, I flipped open one of the books to an illustration that showed a hen, a duck, an owl, and a cat sitting at a table with Little Bear.

"Is it. . . Cat?" I snickered.

Vyz grinned.

"Yes. Although I must confess I'm quite partial to Emily. Their friendship is so innocent and pure. It embodies all the intangible qualities we find so mystifying in mortal children," he said.

I just nodded. The way he spoke almost seemed a little above me at times. Not in a snobby way, just with the speech of someone who'd read millions of stories cover to cover. And more of Bon-Hwa's words came back to me.

"You need more training in wordcraft, royal pet. The first rule of bargaining with fae is never to let the one you want something from name their own price. It is the same as handing over your sword at the start of a duel," she'd said as I sat in her lap.

Motherfucker, she's right. Here I am with the Word Sage, and I've chosen a children's book for a gift, I thought. *He must think me a fool.*

"Sierra? Is something the matter?" he asked.

No hiding my expressions from Varella's brother. I needed to develop some more faces so I'd be less easy for fae to read.

"Just something the queen-in-command told me before we left. Vyz. . . I'm afraid of being a weakness for my mistress. You're both so wise, and you especially know all the words. Your sister disarmed me of my wolfheart one day to illustrate the dangers I'd face in Faerie. And Lady Bon-Hwa showed me the folly in bargaining with her. In truth, they've shown me mercy, but I know how fucked I'd be if I found myself trying to match wits with a redcap or even a piskie."

Especially if that piskie's name rhymes with Godzilla, I thought.

Rubbing his chin again, Vyz looked around at different books. Was there a title he could loan me on wisdom?

"I just. . . I need to find more wisdom, or I'm going to be a liability to my mistress. How do I even begin to accomplish that?" I asked.

Sighing and placing a hand on my shoulder, the lightest touch possible, Vyz looked me deep in the eyes with an expression of reassurance.

"You begin by regaining yourself, Sierra. Ever since your mother died, you've been stripped down to the bare minimum of your soul. Your rotten guardian ground you as though you were an herb in a granite pestle," he said.

Sighing, I found myself agreeing with every word Vyz said. That was a perfect description of what he'd done to me for more than a decade.

"My sister has been rebuilding your heart. I seem to recall one of her intelligence team is helping as well. The road to wisdom starts with being whole. And you need to reclaim yourself. A pot with holes in the side can't hold water. So start with that lost piece of your childhood. Plug a hole. By the time you've finished rediscovering your love for everyone from Grandfather Bear to No Feet, you'll be a little wiser," he said.

It couldn't be that simple, could it? Just. . . re-reading these books my mother used to — no. That's madness. Surely wisdom came from a sacred fountain or a goblet of the ages.

But I didn't want to insult the fae who'd just given me one of the best gifts of my life. And I felt like failing to trust him would be an affront to his kindness.

So. . . I'll get to reading these, I thought.

"Thank you, Vyz. I can't wait to dive back into these," I said.

Stretching and yawning, the elder fae pointed down at my books and said, "Why don't you bind those so they stay together until you return to your home at Featherstone?"

Looking down at the books, I nearly shrugged.

"What. . . do you mean?" I asked. It wasn't like there was a bag at the checkout counter where I could slide these inside.

But the Word Sage had a truth to share here as well.

"I believe my romantic partner gave you the ability to take care of this task when she implanted some of her glamour into your wolfheart," he said.

His romantic partner?! I thought.

The elder fae ignored the look of shock on my face, my eyes the size of dinner plates. Who was his romantic partner?

Pointing at the books again, he said, "Hold the books flat in your hands, one on top, one on bottom."

I did as he instructed.

"Now, picture the books being tied together, not so tight that you damage the covers, but compact enough they don't wiggle as you carry them," he said.

Again, I did as he instructed, not sure what would happen. And at first, nothing happened.

Before I could ask a stupid question, silver ribbons flew from each finger, a delicate-looking lace arranging itself into a neat ornament of stacked books. I didn't even have time to ask what the fuck had just happened as the ribbons tied into a pretty bow on top of the tomes.

My brain sputtered for a moment, trying to figure out where these thin pieces of lace came from. One minute there was nothing, and the next, ribbons flew from the space between each fingertip and nail.

At last, an idea dawned on me as I thought, *Wait. . . I've seen these ribbons before.*

CHAPTER EIGHT

Returning to Featherstone wasn't all that different than initially arriving at Featherbrooke. We passed through Vyz's globe that showed the palace as a miniature structure, and soon we were back inside Varella's room. Or rather, the chamber separating her room from the hallway. I felt a little forlorn leaving Kit and Vyz behind. I wanted more stories from them, more drinks, and more moments.

But Vyzella assured me as my mistress gathered her proposal that I would be returning to Featherbrooke many times in my life.

"You're family," he explained, patting the top of my head softly. "Your title may be royal pet, but you're basically a sister now. Your feet will always find their way to Featherbrooke when you need to, courtesy of the glamour I've imbued them with."

I'd wrapped him in a bone-shattering hug, two seconds away from tears, and thanked him for everything, especially the books. The ribbons binding them together were a constant reminder of my need to have another chat with our queen-in-command.

Now back in Featherstone, I set my books down on a table next to the snow globe with Featherbrooke inside. A tiny flash of lightning arced across the little glass dome. It reminded me of Kit. Gods I already missed that cat. Did HE place any glamour upon me? Because I shouldn't miss him so much.

"My pet? What are you thinking about?" Varella asked, bringing my attention to her. She stood in the middle of the room, facing the door to the hallway. I imagined she had royal duties to attend to upon returning home.

But. . . I wanted more.

As I twiddled my thumbs like a doofus and looked everywhere but my mistress' mesmerizing violet eyes, I struggled to form words.

"Thirty languages in my head, but I don't speak Bottom, darling. You're going to have to use words," she said, setting her proposal down in a nearby chair.

And I must have opened and closed my mouth at least three times before any words came into existence.

"It's just— you were so busy at your brother's house. And then you were asleep. So, I didn't get to spend much time with you. I'm sure you need to reassume the title of queen from Lady Bon-Hwa, but maybe you could delay and instead assume the title of queen of my bedroom?"

Holy shit that sounded stupid, Sierra. Even for you, I thought, swallowing nervously. But that last line appeared to have done the trick because my mistress sauntered over to me, placing two fingers under my chin and raising my eyes to hers.

"Nobody else knows we've returned. But the walk to your bedroom would certainly give our presence away," she said.

I swallowed again.

"Yeah, I suppose you're right," I said, prepared for defeat.

"So I'll have to be the queen of you in my bedroom instead," she whispered, my ears tingling from her voice.

"I've never seen your bedroom before," I said, stupidly twiddling my thumbs again.

Through all of this, I couldn't tear my eyes away from Varella. She just smiled and held my gaze captive as always.

"You've never asked me to fuck you before, either," she said.

And I realized she was right. The queen had fucked me metaphysically since my arrival here, quite a few times. Yet she hadn't physically fucked me, in her words. That was her keeping good on a promise she made shortly after my arrival here that she wouldn't bed me until I asked. So, what the hell? Now was as good a time as any.

"Fuck me, mistress," I said, heart skipping a beat. "Lead me where you will and do with me what you will. I'm ready. I surrender entirely to your charm and desire."

The queen laughed, and it sounded like the dulcet tones of a songbird.

"Let's go, my pet," she said, literally sweeping me off my feet and carrying me into her bedroom bridal style.

I didn't get a chance to look around the bedroom and see what Varella's living space looked like. Of course, it wasn't the queen's living space I was focussed on, but her personal space.

My mistress placed me on a large bed, big enough to hold six people if she wanted a slumber party that large. Black pillows and purple blankets were strewn aside as the seven-foot-tall faerie moved me to the center of the bed.

And then she was on me, lips locked with mine as her taste filled all of my senses. It was raw power, blackberries, and a thorough desire to reduce me to a whimpering puddle of pleasure. My mind swam with every moment she gave me, all of her attention focussed on me here and now. It was like having the attention of a goddess, my personal den of love, impenetrable adoration.

Our lips parted and rejoined a few more times, and the queen pressed her weight upon me, lifting off my top.

She literally snapped her fingers, and my bra dissolved into a pile of black feathers around me. I gasped, and said, "Nice trick."

"You haven't seen anything yet," she said, caressing one of my breasts and running her thumb lightly over the nipple and sending the first shivers of the day down my spine. But I knew more would come.

Varella's cloak fell to the side, and she let me take her top off and unhook her bra the manual way. I found myself surprised at how quickly the fabric surrendered itself to my touch. Or maybe her glamour played a part there as well.

"I hope you understand exactly what you've asked for in a thorough fucking," the queen said, and I felt a heat build between my legs. She'd been there before, plenty of times. But now I could only imagine how much further our lovemaking would go.

She kissed me again and ran her hands over my breasts, squeezing and earning a quick gasp from me as my nipples started to harden a little. She ran her thumbs over each nipple again and again before leaning down and laving my breasts with her tongue. With my head thrown back, a keen raced along my breath, and I squeezed my legs tightly around Varella's waist.

"If you're like putty in my hands, what exactly do you become in my teeth?" Varella laughed before her teeth scraped against my nipple, and I shivered again.

"I'm. . . whatever you want me to be, in your hands, your teeth, your lips, your embrace, your wings, unmake me and make me again 1,000 times between our love," I gushed before kissing my mistress' neck and running my nails down her back.

She sighed and murmured something I couldn't quite hear. Was it a quiet "yes"?

The dark queen of Faerie pulled back and lowered my pants as I felt cool air against my upper hip and thigh.

"My little pet, who is already wet, when we haven't much started yet," the queen said in amusement with her little poem. But she was right. My panties were already damp, and that only grew as the queen pulled them down with her teeth. A promise of more to come?

Raising my hips, so Varella could leave me entirely nude, I whispered, "Please."

Varella's tiny smile revealed her upper hand in this and every situation, which was exactly how I liked it.

"Please what, my pet?" she dared to ask. She dared!

Fuck, I thought. *More teasing?*

And, for one brief moment, the brat broke through as I raised my head at the most taunting angle I could muster, saying, "Please remind me that you know sex requires more than staring."

I almost wished I could've stopped myself. Almost.

But Varella's grin took on the most sinister overshadow I'd ever seen. This was the look of a tiger preparing to pounce and show its victim just how mistaken they were to dare cross paths with an apex predator.

And while I knew my mistress would never hurt me, I knew she was never above putting me in my place.

That was exactly her aim, I realized, as she threw her lips on top of mine again, pushing my head into the pillow, taking my breath away. And at some point, while I was focused on her kiss, Varella's fingers found my lips and started to rub the outsides, beginning a dance that let me know exactly where she was.

Pulling back for just a moment, I heard my mistress say, "You wished for me to remind you about my sexual prowess, is that right?"

The queen's fingers brushed my clit before sliding through my folds and sending a spark through my entire body.

"Well? This was the right spot, correct?" Varella asked as I sighed twice in quick succession. My toes curled as the queen's fingers continued to strike every string on the harp of my fiercely-growing desires.

"Yes," I sputtered, and that took all of my will. Words were quickly falling from my mind as waves of pleasure hit again and again.

My mistress continued to stroke me to the edge of bliss as heat continued to build in my center and spread through my entire body.

"Tell me how much you enjoy being put in your place, my pet," the queen said, knowing I was at her entire mercy, fingers slowing and speeding as she wished, a few moans escaping my lips.

"It's all I want," I hissed through closed teeth.

"Oh, I know. I can tell by how wet you are, how close you are to orgasm. It's not just my touch, but the very understanding of complete surrender to my will that really gets you going, isn't it?" she asked.

I just nodded. Because that *was* what got me going, the idea that she was in control and would break me in half all for my pleasure and her amusement. Throwing my entire fate into her grasp left me breathless and crying for more. Because she was worth giving me over entirely to. It was in the way my mistress looked at me, carrying a hunger for my submission and the awareness of such a deep trust that she'd never let anything bad happen to me.

"What am I to you?" Varella teased as I moaned again.

"Everything," I sighed.

I kissed her again, my tongue dancing through her mouth and reaching for any other part of her I could connect with. More I needed more. I was so close.

"Call me your mistress," she said.

And I did.

"Call me your queen," she said.

And I did.

"Now call me your goddess," she whispered.

My hips bucked as I came against her hand, shivers of radiant felicity charging to every corner of my consciousness, both known and unknown.

"You are my goddess," I said, breathless once more.

Varella leaned close and nibbled on the top of my ear as I hissed.

"We struck a bargain, my pet. And perhaps I'm inclined to grant you another wish. Tell me your desire, little wolf, so that I might know how to unmake you so deeply that only the spark of a great and powerful faerie might put you back together again."

Words. Motions. Acts of pleasure. My mind swam through the current of pleasure she'd washed over me, and I tried to think of something.

At once, it was like someone struck a flare in a pitch-black cave, inspiration dawning on me, my eyes drawn to the glowing red light.

So, pushing my bashfulness aside with all my might, I brought my lips to her ear and whispered something I'd never asked anyone before.

"Restrain me, mistress. And fuck me even harder," I said.

With a small chuckle, my mistress snapped her fingers, and I found my wrists pulled just tight enough in opposite directions that I gasped.

Looking to the right, I found one of my wrists bound with a thin black rope tied to part of Varella's bed frame.

When I pulled, it held steady, but with no burn or friction upon my flesh. It was as if the rope was simultaneously made of the world's most powerful fibers and the softest silk. My other arm was restrained similarly. And Varella? Well, she just waited there for a moment before whispering, "If at any point this gets to be too much, quickly say my name three times. We'll stop immediately."

I nodded, renewed buzz flooding my body. I'd never been restrained before and didn't even imagine it in my most twisted fantasies. But that's exactly what my mistress left me wanting. . . twisted fantasies.

Without warning, Varella ran the flat of her tongue up my center, and I didn't so much gasp as I. . . fuck. What was a more powerful expression than a gasp? Well, make up whatever word you want and use it. Because that's what I did.

I pulled tight at the ropes, and the bed frame groaned as my back bowed. That's when the tip of Varella's tongue flicked against my clit, and I was reduced to a puddle of senseless and baffling noises. Words? Consonants? Vowels? All gone.

Head empty. No thoughts. Only a deluxe joy, the likes of which I'd never known before.

"My goodness, the way you just seem to grow more wet. It's like I'm drowning over here. We could annihilate all the deserts in the world with this much moisture," she said.

And before I could say something bratty in response, the queen explored all I had to offer with her lips and tongue, fireworks exploding all over my body, behind my eyes, at the center of my mind, up and down my thighs. It was electrifying, and as my mistress grew even more bold in her exploration, I yelled, "Fuck! Yes, take me. Take me down, Varella."

That's exactly what the queen did as I curled my toes and a wet heat engulfed my fingertips. My skin felt hot to the touch, and I wanted the queen to smother me with her cool, dark glamour and send me over the edge into complete euphoria.

"Don't stop. I'm so close again," I said.

But the queen needed no instructions, because she knew me, and understood exactly where I was. I had no secrets or mysteries kept from her. I wasn't just an open book before her, but a spread of pages across the table, all my words spilled free for her to see.

My mistress' lips wrapped around my clit and sucked, her tongue flicking quickly and hard against the nerve bundle.

I'm going to pass out, I thought, never before having experienced such a passionate ravishing.

"Fuck," I shouted again and came once more.

Lying there and shivering with an infinite pleasure that seemed to take me outside of time itself, I wrapped my arms around Varella who crawled on top of me and kissed me with a mixture of my juices and her own.

Wait, my hands are free, I thought, realizing that I wasn't entirely sure when that happened.

But I found myself eager to please and somehow used my remaining strength to flip Varella over and bring my fingers to her fold.

"Oh!" she gasped, as I danced around her folds, extracting a patient pleasure from my mistress. But I wasn't going to just ring the bell. I was going into the house to make it my own, as she had for me.

Pushing my fingers inside, I felt the queen buckle, eyes closed, and teeth drawn tight into a smile.

My fingers curled in exploration until they found a spot that made the queen squirm beneath me, one knee rising above the other with a quick moan.

I didn't let up, and I got the feeling that my touch was hitting the queen like a lightning strike as I continued to play. She shook, and I found myself growing wet again from knowing I was bringing her along on this journey.

My fingers firmed and pressed against a spot I knew the queen could never reach by herself.

"Sierra, yes," she said, trembling as I brought her to the edge.

"Sierra yes, indeed," I smiled as her legs drew up reflexively, Varella's fingers tangling in my hair.

As she squirmed and came against my hand, the queen's eyelids fluttered. Her chest swelled as she inhaled and exhaled in happiness.

Licking my fingers in front of the queen, she opened her eyes, and I saw renewed vulnerability for just a second. Yet another face, one of great promise, an oath that she'd never leave me. And by extension, I'd never be allowed to leave her. But that was just fine because she was all I wanted and more.

The brat in me grinned evilly in mistaken confidence while I was on top of the queen. Licking my fingers again, I looked down upon the queen and said, "Submit."

Without warning, I was flung to the right and caught in the crook of her arm, falling back to the bed. Then the queen climbed on top of me and started to gradually trib.

"Oh fuck. Oh fuck!" I hissed, renewed fireworks picking right up where she left off when Varella had been on top.

"No, Sierra. You will submit. Never mistake my allowance for your pleasuring me to be a sign of submission. I am the queen, and you are my. . ." she trailed off, grinding a little harder.

I convulsed, caught entirely in her grasp. And surrender quickly became my only option as the words in my brain faded into the glowing sensation of her complete ownership, of me, of this room, of this situation.

"Your pet," I whispered.

She moved harder against me, and I tried to match her tempo and pressure.

"Say it," she said. "Say you submit."

Our scissoring took on a higher gear than even I thought possible, and unsurprisingly, when I could hold back no more, I came for a third time, orgasm rocking my mind so much that it might as well move in and split the rent with my subconsciousness.

"I submit," I somehow found the air to say. "I'll always submit to you, mistress."

At that point, the queen kissed my forehead and said, "Good girl."

Then she moved her head down to rest on my breasts, and I wrapped my arms around Varella, cuddling until one or both of us drifted off into a mid-morning nap.

CHAPTER NINE

Sleep held me for just a little longer than my mistress as my mind swam through sheets of silk and the smell of her bosom I was buried in. But eventually, the afternoon light penetrated my eyelids and gradually roused me from my slumber.

When my brain finally started making sense, I realized that no matter which way my arms reached, the queen was nowhere to be found. And, in fact, the light placement was wrong. I could tell by where the light shined through the windows that I was not in the queen's bed but my own.

As my eyes finally parted, and a blurry visage of my bedroom passed into my line of sight, I slowly sat up and yawned.

"Well, finally. I didn't think it was normal for mortals to sleep so late in the day, but with every moment you call this home I learn more," a familiar piskie's voice called from across my bedroom.

Turning and trying to focus my eyes, I caught sight of Barsilla sitting over on my armoire, legs crossed and dangling over the edge. My copy of A Kiss for Little Bear was open in front of her, floating in the air.

"Hey, please be careful with those," I said, voice a little more raspy than I expected.

While I cleared my throat, the piskie snapped her fingers, and the book gently flew back down to the stack and closed, perfectly in line with the others.

"I assure you, I was careful. Mother Bear can be a bit of a bitch to her cub. I like her," the piskie said, flying across my room with buzzing little wings on her back.

Looking over at the books, I nodded, still trying to wake up. I found myself tired. . . but in a good way? Like I had just enough grogginess hanging around my mind and body to remind me of this morning's activities, but it felt welcome, almost like a nice buzz or a gentle high.

"Sorry, Barsilla. I just can't quite seem to wake up entirely. It's like there's a. . . tiny and pleasant chill stuck to my subconscious. But I feel it in my muscles, too," I said, touching the space on my neck where the queen had marked me.

The piskie landed on my bed frame and nodded.

"Well, that's to be expected after a complete and thorough shellacking our queen gave you this morning. I'm sure you had fun, but in some ways making love to her is like making love to an electric wire in your world. Your body is going to hum for a little bit afterward, all that magic and energy you exchanged."

She paused for a moment and looked me up and down.

"Your body is running on a glamour high. She already has a large chunk of her power in your wolfheart, but after what you two did earlier, you're practically smothered in her aura. A normal human would probably go to sleep and never wake up again. But you werewolves are remarkably durable. You just keep bouncing back so long as silver isn't involved."

I guess that made sense. Our activities had been. . . quite thorough and explicit. My body still shivered just remembering it all.

"How long will this feeling last?" I asked, rubbing my eyes. "Not that I'm eager to get rid of it. It's. . . pretty relaxing."

As I said that, another chill ran down my arm, causing goosebumps.

Barsilla looked me over again. She then started counting on her fingers as if this was some kind of complex equation I didn't understand. Not mortal math, that's for sure.

"I'd say you should be back to feeling normal before bed tonight. Maybe watch your abilities today. Don't try to make use of the queen's glamour embedded within you until all this excess aura disperses. Who knows what madness would be unleashed?"

That was fine by me. I didn't have another training session with Ceras until tomorrow anyway. And we were still working mostly on forms and stances. We hadn't even gotten to tapping into the queen's glamour. I hadn't used it much since summoning that pack of feather wolves to defend the palace from the lake witch.

I wasn't eager to tap into that power again. In the week after the lakeshore battle, which I spent recovering from being stabbed in the gut, my body felt all kinds of weird. Using an immortal's magic in a mortal body just felt like mixing mayonnaise and peanut butter. It's possible, but the taste is pretty funky.

"Speaking of glamour, to get at your books, I had to pull off a couple ribbons. And I couldn't help but notice they seemed a little familiar. . .," Barsilla said, staring at me out of the corner of her eyes.

"Yeah, I've got questions about that, myself. But I won't know anything for sure until I talk to Lady Bon-Hwa," I said, staring at my fingers.

Barsilla hovered in the air again and snapped her fingers. The door to my bathroom opened, and I heard the bath kick on inside. Somehow I knew the temperature would be exactly where I wanted it, which had me curious about just how far Barsilla's intuition went.

She snapped her fingers again, and a pair of soft white towels flew from out of the bathroom and onto my bed.

"You're in luck, little wolf. Our queen in command is awaiting your arrival for lunch. So you might just get a chance to ask those questions after all."

I started to get out of bed and then paused, staring at Barsilla with an eyebrow raised.

"What did I say about calling me little wolf when you're less than six inches tall?" I asked, crossing my arms.

She didn't even flinch.

"What did I say about telling me what to do when I could shrink you down to the size of a grape and then cut you into five pieces with the snap of my fingers?" the piskie asked, putting her hands on those microscopic hips of hers.

We continued to glare at each other in awkward silence, and eventually, I lost the contest, same as always.

"I'm. . . going to go get in the bath," I said, clearing my throat and grabbing the towels.

"Excellent choice, royal pet," Barsilla said, flying back over to my Little Bear books to finish the one she'd been reading.

I called out.

"Those are very important to me. So again, please be careful," I said.

Before I closed the bathroom door, I heard Barsilla's voice soften a tad as she said, "I know who gave you these and how dear they are to you. They'll be just fine in my care for the few minutes I'll need to read them."

Strangely enough, I trusted her. So I bathed quickly, found a new soap that smelled like black raspberries, and rinsed off.

Selecting a yellow and orange sundress, I got dressed, put on a little makeup, and left my room to find Lady Bon-Hwa.

I stopped one of the queen's feathers, a troll with a surprisingly thick German accent, and asked if he'd seen the queen in command. The troll pointed a large hand covered in gray flesh toward the rear of the castle and said she was outside near the water's edge.

Thanking the feather and leaving, I hummed to myself and wandered through the palace until I came to the rear doorway. Outside, several feathers stood guard and waved to me as I walked by. The talon in command was an elf named Belamie, and she looked a little nervous as I exited the grounds without an escort. She'd been nearby when I ran out before, and the queen gave chase.

Nobody was scolded for that, of course. Ornery werewolves are notoriously difficult to stop, as I knew from experience. Still, none of the feathers or talons wanted to be caught on the end of the queen's wrath if something happened to her favorite puppy — er, wolf. I was her werewolf. I had to keep at least some measure of respect for myself.

Just because Barsilla calls me that doesn't mean I need to start, I thought, rolling my eyes.

I found Lady Bon-Hwa just outside of the palace staring at the lake, her long black hair drifting along with the breeze coming off the water. As usual, her hair was tied back with a ribbon, this one a soft blue.

The queen in command wore a matching form-fitting little blue dress that looked like someone a hiker would wear, along with black tights underneath. I didn't know fae seamstresses could make or use polyester.

Maybe Bon-Hwa hit up an L.L.BEAN store before asking me to lunch, I thought.

"There you are, little wolf. I was wondering when you would wake up," she said as I noticed a wicker picnic basket in her hands.

"My apologies, Lady Bon-Hwa. I didn't know we were having lunch today. You could have always asked Barsilla to wake me up," I said.

The queen in command smiled.

"No, I've heard it's best to let sleeping dogs lie. . . isn't that the expression in the mortal world?"

Snickering, I nodded.

"Plus, I know your body needed to rest after your mistress fucked you to Avalon and back," Bon-Hwa said with a straight face.

And there they went again. My cheeks were burning something fierce. I wasn't ashamed of what we'd done. I rather enjoyed myself. So why did I still blush like an embarrassed teenager when other people talked about my sex life? Maybe it was just the manner in which it was discussed.

Perhaps I'll never get used to the blunt nature that folks here use to talk about my explicit activities, I thought.

Then again, it wasn't like the fae were prudes. Pleasure was something the inhabitants of this world seemed to know everything about. They did things here mortals didn't even have names for back where I came from. It was in the same ballpark as desire, seduction, dancing, passion, and all the other things fae spent their limitless days seeking out.

"I didn't think we were that noisy," I said, clearing my throat.

Bon-Hwa shook her head.

"No, dear. We certainly didn't hear the two of you. Varella's bedroom is enchanted with all kinds of magic to keep her secrets safe in the dark. But most of us saw her carrying you back to your bedroom. And you're still dripping with her glamour. So, everyone in Featherstone can do the math."

Speaking of, my mind still had its buzz going from being overloaded on my mistress' aura, so I swayed to the left a little with the lake breeze.

"I trust you've recovered enough to walk a little ways for a picnic?"

Staring again at the basket and wondering what goodies were inside, I asked, "Why did you choose now for us to share a meal?"

Why indeed? I'd never pretend like I could guess Bon-Hwa's true intentions, but this one should have been obvious enough.

"To uphold our bargain, of course. I told you that after your trip to Featherbrooke, I'd show you my true face. So. . . here I am," she said, motioning around herself with an arm.

Right, we'd made a bargain. How could I have forgotten? It was just a couple days ago, but somehow after meeting Kit and Vyz, it felt longer than that.

"Well, okay then. In that case, I'm sorry I forgot. By all means, let's eat lunch. I'm eager to see the true Lady Bon-Hwa."

The queen in command seemed to glance out at the lake again and then motioned for me to follow her into the forest.

We hiked for what felt like an hour, maybe two. But time was always an enigma in the land of Faerie. That was to be expected for a race of beings that simply marched outside the flow of chronology.

Eventually, we came to a patch of flat rocks next to a small waterfall. It fed into a river that I assumed went out into the lake surrounded Featherstone. It was here Bon-Hwa finally sat down the picnic basket and pulled out a thick blanket. I helped her spread it over the largest rock in the area, and we got to eating pretty quickly after that.

The queen in command had the kitchen prepare several roasted chicken sandwiches that were served cold. And I wasn't sure if Varella had told her about my appetite or she just naturally guessed werewolves at more than the average person. But every time I reached into the basket to pull out another sandwich, one appeared.

Lady Bon-Hwa put away two sandwiches before wiping her mouth with a cloth napkin from the basket and looking over at the waterfall.

"I'm not sure what you're expecting to see, royal pet."

Thinking back on our last exchange, I remembered falling drastically short of the queen in command's expectations where wordcraft was concerned. And I'd learned my lesson about folly. What if this was another test on her part?

I need to ace it, I thought.

Putting my half-eaten sandwich down, I folded my hands in my lap and spoke slowly, as if trying to verbally feel around my bedroom with the lights off.

"You promised to show me your true face and told me I craved expressions of authenticity here, that it was my mortal nature. So that is what I expect, my lady. An authentic expression of your true face," I said, my eyes trying to flash confidence.

The fae appraised my look with an analytical eye that probably took centuries to develop. And I sensed she knew I was full of bullshit. But she just nodded twice and said, "Good. That's a little better. It seems like your visit to the Word Sage helped after all."

Before I could argue that nothing much had changed, I remembered what Vyz had told me about gaining wisdom.

"The road to wisdom starts with being whole. And you need to reclaim yourself. A pot with holes in the side can't hold water. So start with that lost piece of your childhood," he'd told me in the library.

He'd given me back a small piece of my childhood with those books. Could the simple act of knowing I had such a treasure waiting for me to read at any time count as reclaiming myself? And the bigger question. . . did that necessarily give me any extra wisdom?

Clearing my throat and trying to push aside that squeamish feeling that reared its head anytime I had to be assertive, I blinked slowly and said, "I can tell you all about my visit to Vyz and Kit later. But I believe we hiked out here for a reason. And I'd like to see your true face, my lady."

At that moment Bon-Hwa's eyes seemed to darken a shade, and she dropped the complimentary mask that said nice words and revealed a more terrifying sight. Externally, she was still the same otherworldly beauty that I'd walked into the woods with. But inside, the queen in command's aura changed and seemed to raise as though a viper from its nest in the ground.

My skin shivered as gooseflesh appeared, and she knew the subtle shift in her demeanor hadn't gone unnoticed.

This look she wore now was. . . I'd describe it as visceral and hungry. Her eyes were wild and focussed on one thing at this very moment. . . myself.

There was a controlled rage present now, something that had been invisible below the surface. I didn't know the source of this acrimony, but I didn't have to wait for it to be revealed.

"Well, little wolf. Congratulations. You're maybe the third person in the Raven Court to see my true face, my unbridled hunger for power. My face comes with a short backstory. It starts with a girl who became a slave at a young age and learns all the brutality of the world. Your pampered life here may give you an ignorant view of Faerie, but make no mistake, this is a cold, animalistic world full of spiteful creatures ready to throw you in the mud and drive daggers into your spine."

I swallowed nervously and exhaled slowly.

"That story continues with the little girl furnishing a new hatred for her owners each day, until they finally let their guard down, putting her in charge of their meals. Their deaths came via poison and ribbons that I used to squeeze the last bit of life from their previously immortal bodies. This face came from an insatiable urge to rise up and tear as much power and glamour from Faerie as I could imagine and more," she hissed.

My chest felt tight, and the buzz from earlier seemed to evaporate from fear, fear of this raw and true face, the very face I'd asked to see. Except now that I saw it, I wanted to look anywhere else.

But I didn't. I held her gaze, not wanting to disrespect the expression of her truest self. This is what I'd bargained for. And it was what I now received. It was the very foundation of Lady Bon-Hwa.

"And now you're the second-most powerful fae in the Raven Court. That's quite a jump from slave, my lady," I all but stuttered.

Her eyes narrowed, but it did nothing to lessen the enmity in her gaze.

"It's nothing compared to the jump I'll make as queen of the Raven Court. That's my endgame, little wolf. The corvid crown is what drives me morning, day, and night, growing my glamour and eventually seizing a throne so that nobody will ever again be able to order me around."

With this confession, her glamour spread to the stones around us, and ribbons rose like snakes, numbering a dozen. They filled spaces between the rocks as though they'd been slumbering here throughout our picnic.

And then the ribbons wrapped around each rock, most of which were the size of a human desk or chair. When Lady Bon-Hwa squeezed her fist, the ribbons joined together and fastened themselves around nearby rocks, squeezing tight until the stone groaned and shattered into pieces before my eyes.

The very air itself became thick with Lady Bon-Hwa's glamour. I felt it pulse around the stream and stones as though it was hunting. Because she was hunting. . . for the crown of my mistress.

At that moment, something snapped inside me, and a deep growl rattled the now-shattered rocks around us. My fear of the queen in command faded, replaced with renewed loyalty to my mistress.

"You seek the crown of our queen, Lady Bon-Hwa?"

She didn't seem fazed in the least at my rattling growl, merely standing until the powerful fae towered over me.

"I've made no secret of my desire to the Raven Queen, and now I reveal this secret to you as well. My service to the queen is all in preparation for sitting on her throne myself one day."

"Treason!" I barked, standing on my own feet and clenching my fists. To threaten to supplant my mistress was an action I wouldn't tolerate. I've no clue what the queen in command thought bringing out here and telling me this, but I was going to put a stop to anything she was planning here and now.

But with a flick of her wrist, I found myself raised several inches into the air, ribbons securing my wrists and ankles, another at my throat.

"Consider this another lesson, little wolf. Be careful who you bark at. I could tear you into tiny pieces in the blink of an eye or across the longest hour you've ever known. And you—" I interrupted her, feeling glamour stirring in my wolfheart.

The thought of seeing harm come to my queen while I just stood here in the woods sparked across my chest like a bolt of lightning.

"Will defend my queen until you've ripped every last breath from my lungs," I said.

Glamour pushed outward from my chest as I visualized them around me, the ones I hadn't called in a few months. Razor focus and need summoned them to me once again.

But the ribbons around me pulled tighter, not that I let even a groan slip as my tendons began to protest.

"Empty threats and bravado may accomplish things in the mortal world. But this is Faerie, royal pet. And I have you alone in the woods hanging in the air before me helpless as a bug in a web."

With another growl, I matched the queen in command's fierce gaze. Words flashed through my mind. Traitor. Usurper. Conspirator. I didn't care if she was the second-most powerful fae in the Raven Court. I wouldn't let her take one step toward my mistress.

"Not alone," I said.

"What was that?" she asked, holding up a hand to her ear. She'd heard me, knew exactly what I'd said.

But I didn't have to repeat myself because a twig snapped behind us. And that's when she turned to see us surrounded by a dozen wolves made entirely from blackened leaves and feathers, violet eyes glowing and locked onto the queen in command.

Now it wasn't just my growl filling the air with Varella's glamour spilling from my chest, but the entire black feather pack.

These were the same wolves I'd called to fight the invading force of kelpies attacking Featherstone. And I was beginning to understand exactly what it would take to summon them again and again.

Lady Bon-Hwa now wore a sickening grin as she gazed at the pack around us. Then she turned her back on them and looked back at me.

Maybe her animosity cooled a degree or two. Maybe that was my imagination. But the fae before me nodded twice more.

"Good," she said. "Very good."

I pulled against my bonds until I started to feel my bones groaning as the stones did earlier when her ribbons snaked around them. I leaned my head forward and answered her true face with my own.

"Look at me, Lady Bon-Hwa. This is my true face. These are my claws and fangs. I am the goddamn Wolf of Featherstone and the loyal pet of her majesty Varella. I serve her with everything I've got. I will for all my years. You might kill me here. You might take down this black feather pack. But know two things. You won't leave this forest unscathed, and my spirit will forever hunt you through whatever eternity you have left."

Her face changed, and that deranged, power-hungry expression retreated behind a calmer mask, one I couldn't immediately place. With another flick of her wrist, the ribbons that broke stones apart only moments ago cracked like whips, destroying every black feather wolf I'd summoned.

As those feathers and leaves fell back to the ground from which I'd summoned them, I felt the ribbons holding me slack a little until I was back on my own feet.

"That's the face you'll need when our queen takes you to Kilgara in a few days. So remember this feeling well, royal pet. Remember how it felt to summon those creatures with the use of her majesty's glamour inside of you. And for crow's sake, learn to harness the glamour I planted in your wolfheart as well."

I cocked my head to the side, feeling fury inside my heart evaporating like rain from the pavement on a hot summer day.

"Here is the last truth I will share with you today, little wolf. My service to the queen started decades before even your grandmother was born. And it began with an oath that I wouldn't pursue the corvid crown while she still wore it. Do I crave your mistress' power? Yes. Do I know how to keep those cravings in check until my time arrives? Also yes. So turn that protective force outward, and don't make any more foolish bargains."

In truth, I wasn't sure how to feel at the moment. I'd been prepared to tear Lady Bon-Hwa's heart out seconds ago, and now I was taking final pieces of advice from her.

Things change quickly in the land of Faerie. I guess that's all I could say.

"Then. . . this *was* a test," I said, raising an eyebrow.

"It was," she said, closing the picnic basket and folding the blanket we'd sat on. I watched her stand and start back on the path toward Featherstone.

Following alongside the queen in command, I asked, "Did I pass?"

She said nothing for a few seconds before looking down my way with a coy grin. And I knew the time of her giving answers had passed.

"That'll do, wolf. That'll do."

I guess that's all I'm going to get from her, I thought as we continued our hike back to the palace.

CHAPTER TEN

Heading back from axe combat training with Ceras, I detoured and headed to the lakeshore instead of the palace. Though I was right outside the gate, I wasn't too interested in heading inside yet.

I wanted to sit in the sand and grass and wait to see if a ship carrying my girlfriend would sail by. It'd been a few weeks since Lily left Perth by boat for an assignment in the Tulip Court, and I'd missed her terribly since.

My bed was awful lonely, and I missed the late-night conversations we used to stay up and have, legs intertwined as we shared a chair and ate popcorn together.

Of course, I loved finally getting to spend some time with the queen as she'd been busy working on her proposal for Bliss. But Lily was a different kind of energy, and she occupied a separate piece of my heart, one that ached for her.

Pulling my legs up to my chest, I remembered that we'd be leaving for Kilgara, where every court in Faerie would meet on neutral ground while the rulers of each land decided who would host the upcoming Bliss.

I was to remain in my wolf form the entire time from the moment we left Featherstone until we returned for my protection of course. Supposedly, I would be harder to attack or capture when I weighed 200 pounds and had razor-sharp fangs and claws.

And I'm sure my inner wolf would appreciate the long spur to stretch her legs as we traveled beside the queen and put every wandering stare her way in its place.

That was two days from now, of course. And now. . . was now. In the moment, my heart, a piece of it, anyway, felt lonely. It missed the fae that connected with me on a more human level than the maelstrom of glamour that was her majesty.

While I sat there watching the occasional redeye buckfish leap from the water to catch a dragonfly on the surface, I heard a certain piskie approaching from the palace.

Barsilla's wings buzzed as she flew around and into view, carrying the little clipboard she always had with her.

"Oh, hey Barsilla. Did you need something?" I asked, lifting my chin from my arms where it'd been resting while I sat there.

Varella's left-hand lady cocked her head to the side, looked down at some tiny scribbling she had, and then stared back up at me.

"Ceras mentioned you seemed extra moody during your combat training today, and now I find you out here moping by the lake."

I raised an eyebrow.

"I'm not moping," I said, with all the convincing tone of a teenager stamping her foot. "I'm just. . . resting after a hard workout. That's not illegal in the Raven Court, is it?"

Barsilla rolled her eyes like a mother dealing with a sulking teen. Dammit, why was that suddenly all I could think about?

"Your mortal emotions aren't something the queen can afford to be distracted by right now, especially not with the summit coming up. And make no mistake, she will be distracted if she catches you moping. So, you might as well tell me what's wrong so I can waste my time fixing it and avoid any diversions on the queen's part," the piskie said.

I let out a sigh and turned my attention back to the lake because my problem was simple to describe and impossible for Barsilla to fix. . . unless her magic included the ability to summon my girlfriend at the drop of a hat.

"I miss Lily. That's all," I said, putting my chin back down.

Barsilla opened her mouth and then closed it again. She thought before speaking, but I don't think it did her a lot of good because she was still going to inevitably be a jerk about this.

"By the gods, you're such a needy puppy!"

Then she rolled her eyes a second time.

"But that is a problem easily fixed. Follow me," she said, and I stood, wondering what she intended to do.

Barsilla led me back inside the palace and to a room I'd never seen before. Feathers stood outside the room protecting it, but they slid aside for Barsilla and me without a word.

The room was filled with paintings of ravens, crows, and magpies. Some sat in trees, some by rivers, and others under bushes, scavenging for fallen nuts and berries. There must have been about 20 paintings in different styles ranging from lifelike portraits to impressionist scenes.

"What is this place?" I asked, still looking around at all the artwork.

"This is the Hall of Winged Messengers. Our queen will sometimes use these birds to contact others discreetly," Barsilla said, coming to rest in the seat of a large red velvet chair.

"She uses. . . the paintings to talk to other people?" I asked, scratching the back of my head and trying to picture how that would work.

Varella's left-hand lady shook her head. But I did notice that she didn't roll her eyes this time. That was progress. . . for me anyway. I tended to ask a lot of stupid questions. Or at least, questions faeries would find ignorant because I didn't know any better.

Deciding to teach by example, Barsilla instructed me to select a bird and walk over to the painting it sat in. I still didn't know what the hell I was doing, so I found a magpie with black and white feathers and blue-tipped wings. The painting it sat in showed the bird huddled between several wildflowers, perhaps hunting for something to make a nest with.

"Hold out your hand in front of the bird and say, 'Queen Varella commands you to carry my words.'"

I wasn't sure what would happen, but I slowly held out my right hand in front of the painting, palm up flat. Then I said, "Queen Varella commands you to carry my words."

At first, nothing happened. And I gave Barsilla a look of suspicion. Was she making a joke of me? It would be like the fae to pull a prank like this on a mortal unfamiliar with their ways.

She just motioned that I turn back to the painting. When I did, a magpie hopped off the canvas, suddenly springing to life in a three-dimensional world. It flew off the artwork as if the oil paint was being rewound in time, returning to its paintbrush.

But instead of turning back into paint, the animal kept its form and hopped down into my open hand. I felt its thin twig-like talons hop across my hand as its head tilted from side to side. The bird looked like it was waking up from a long hibernation. Then it glanced up at me with its red eyes, black dotted pupils focussed directly on my face.

Looking back at the canvas, I noticed the bird missing from its scenery. Only the wildflowers and sky remained.

The magpie continued to hop around in my hand, stretching its wings and turning its head this way and that.

"I. . . is this a real bird?" I asked, looking at the piskie that was just half the magpie's size sitting across the room from me.

She hovered closer, and I expected the animal to see her as prey given their size difference. But the magpie made no move to leave my hand.

"That bird is made from the queen's glamour, as you carry in your wolfheart. Only those with her majesty's magic can call forth these birds and send them out into the world," Barsilla said, motioning to the other ravens and crows. It was a room full of carrion callers.

Despite my expectations that the bird would start chirping or cawing in some way, I found the animal strangely silent. It might occasionally look away, but otherwise, the magpie seemed to do nothing more than observe me.

"So. . . how does this work exactly?" I asked. "Am I going to write a message on a tiny piece of paper, and this magpie will carry it to Lily? Like on Game of Thrones?"

Barsilla furrowed her brow.

"This isn't a game, pet. And you don't need to use a throne to send your message either. I swear, you mortals say the weirdest things. The first thing you need to do is hold the magpie up to your chest."

"Why?"

"So it can hear who your heart beats for, who you want to send a message to. I still find it strange that not only does our queen have a soft spot for a mortal, but she's also willing to share her puppy with her subordinate. Still, it's not my place to question her," Barsilla said.

I slowly held the magpie up to my chest as instructed. Part of me felt like I was still being pranked. But the magpie just hopped over to my pinky finger and placed its ear against my breast, closing its eyes and listening to my heartbeat.

"I will question you, royal pet. Describe for me your heart when you think of Lily. Then tell me how it compares to when you think about your mistress. I simply can't imagine being in love with both of them, a queen, and a spy," Barsilla asked.

When the bird was finished listening to my heartbeat, it skipped back into the center of my palm and started watching me again, presumably waiting for whatever message I was going to give the bird to carry.

And it wasn't bad enough that I had to figure out the exact words I wanted to send to Lily. I had to answer prying questions from Barsilla about my feelings? Fuck. Even I didn't understand my feelings half the time.

Polyamory was a new thing for me. Being gay took me long enough to understand. I mean — I understood on some level what it meant to look at girls in my high school and think, *Fuck, she's so pretty.*

The way talking to a crush left my heart jogging in place like it was warming up for a marathon took weeks and months to sort out. Then I had to try to figure out if a girl felt the same way about me, and fuck was that even more difficult.

But I did figure it out eventually.

Now here I was still trying to figure out how to love two women at the same time when each made my heart quiver in different ways. They made other parts of me quiver as well. But that was neither here nor there.

And Barsilla wanted, what? An essay on how they made me feel? Shit. I'd have an easier time lecturing her on quantum physics.

"What do you want me to say?" I asked.

"I want you to tell me how two fae ladies I've known for much longer than you make a werewolf howl in heat," Barsilla said.

I scoffed. No way was I telling the piskie things Varella and Lily had done to make me howl in ecstasy. But the more I thought about it, I realized she wasn't asking about deeds, but emotions.

Fae weren't like mortals. Their understanding of our emotions and motivations was limited to what they observed when they took a vacation in the realm where time still flows.

That's part of the reason I connected so deeply to Lily. She was half-human, and that meant it was easier to talk to her about my fears and dreams, really lay them out on the bed sheets in front of her. And she understood. Gods, she understood. Maybe that was what Barsilla wanted here. . . to understand.

"Well. . . Lily — see — she makes me feel like there's no one in the world except for us when we're together. Like reality and all its problems and the people who make them are so far removed because she's taken my hand and guided me to a place of gentle love and sweetness."

The piskie wrote something down on her clipboard and nodded.

"And your mistress? How does she make you feel?"

Taking a deep breath, I considered the morning we'd had a couple days ago.

"My mistress. . . she makes me feel like I'm in the eye of a hurricane. All the power in the world to destroy anything that tries to do me harm while I'm kept safe and sound at the center of the storm. With her, I feel like I'm going to be swept away at any moment, but when it happens, the place I'll be swept to is in her arms. And I trust that whether I'm on the ground or in the sky she'll protect me."

Barsilla smiled as she took more notes.

"What was all that about?" I asked, cocking my head to the side like the magpie in my hand.

She finished writing something and then looked back up at me.

"Now you know exactly how you feel about each of them. No more wishy-washy shit humans do. Treasure each with the full confidence that you can love two people at the same time and be cherished by each simultaneously."

With that, she started to fly over toward the door. Barsilla stopped just before opening the exit and looked back my way.

"When you're ready to send your message, hold the magpie up into your direct gaze and speak to it as if it were Lily. The moment you look away or lose focus, it'll fly away to carry your message, regardless of whether you were finished."

Then, Varella's left-hand lady left me alone with the magpie. I felt a little nervous about getting my message cut off. It didn't take much to distract me. I suppose that was something I had in common with the corvid I was holding. My brain could think, *shiny!* at a moment's notice. Perhaps that's how I fell in love with two different faeries in the first place.

But instead of getting distracted, I thought about my girlfriend, the lesbian faerie I missed cuddling with every single night, the gay girl who wasn't just part of my dreams, but my waking world as well.

Holding up the magpie about a foot from my face, I looked deep into its crimson eyes and said:

"Dear Lily, I miss you more than you can know. And I hope the bird that tracks you down over in the Tulip Court doesn't make me sound too clingy. I've yet to see how fae react to clinginess. But in case it's negative, do me a favor and pretend this message is a lot more breezy and cool than it actually is.

"Featherstone feels lonely without you. I'm happy when I'm with my mistress, but in other moments, my heart pines for the girl who plays board games with me in my room and holds me close when I bolt awake after a nightmare about my father until I come back to reality, safe and sound.

"But I know your mission is important. I would never ask you to come home early and risk disappointing our queen. So, instead, I'll just ask two things. First, think of me in the moments when that mask you wear feels a little too tight and smothering. Remember that I'm here waiting for you in a place where you just get to be Lily, my girlfriend. Not a wing for the Raven Court. Second, come back to me safely. Because even though I know you've been doing this for years, and you're the best spy my mistress has. . . I might still worry.

"Oh, and bring me back a cool Tulip Court souvenir if you can. Maybe a tulip? Actually — scratch that, magpie.

That's three things, and I said I'd only ask two. Seriously. Don't repeat this part to my girlfriend. It'll make me look stupid, like I don't know how to use a winged messenger. So . . . you're not gonna say this last part, right?"

I was interrupted by the sound of Barsilla's raucous laughter coming from outside in the hallways and looked away for a split second, fearing she'd overheard me.

When I looked back, only a single black and white feather remained in my hand.

"Aw, shit."

CHAPTER ELEVEN

Walking into a dimly lit basement, I looked down at the cracked concrete floor. The room smelled of old drainage and expired cleaning products. I turned around to see the mirror I'd just crawled out of and caught sight of the Intrinsic Pathways chamber fading back into my reflection.

A simple white plastic border surrounded the glass surface. The thing was barely big enough for me to fit through. Barsilla didn't have any trouble, though — the benefit of being a piskie and only a few inches tall.

She darted up to my shoulder and hid herself in my hair.

"I'm glad you've been growing your hair out," she said.

A moment later, the piskie stuck her head out of my hair and added, "And I'm also glad you switched to the pineapple and raspberry shampoo."

I rolled my eyes. Today I was playing carriage to the queen's left-hand lady in the human world. And I could already tell it was going to be a test of my nerves. I'd never spent an extended time with Barsilla before, primarily because she was a bit scolding and judgmental.

But today came with an important mission before we left for Kilgara tomorrow. We needed to make contact with a powerful fae that lived in the human world.

"How can a fae live in the human world full-time? Wouldn't that be a death sentence with all the iron and the lack of glamour?" I'd asked my queen.

"You'll see," was all she said before sending me here to accompany Barsilla. And by accompany, she meant carry.

The piskie looked around the little room we'd appeared in. It was a small space with concrete walls and floors. A shelf of cleaning suppliesstood against one wall, along with a mop and a janitor's cart on wheels.

"Where are we?" I asked.

A grimy voice from the ceiling made me jump. I looked around to find the source.

"You're in the basement of Ssorc Insurance Arena," a masculine-presenting fae said. When I finally found him, my eyes widened.

In one of the ceiling corners hung a spider-like faery about a foot tall. When I got a closer look, I saw he had the body of a tiny man but also a thorax and four narrow legs behind him that clung to the wall.

His front arms were crossed as he looked down at us. Eight brown and black eyes spread across his forehead kept a close watch on us.

"Hello there," he said, waving a tiny hand. "Name's Jello. Welcome to Portland."

I raised a finger and opened my mouth to speak.

"Because he likes to eat Jell-O," Barsilla said from inside my hair.

I lowered my finger and closed my mouth, nodding. That made plenty of sense. Maybe I could change my name to Chicken Nugget.

"You're not going to come out and say hello to your old friend, Barsilla?" Jello called with a grin, revealing two fangs and additional mandibles.

Her voice called out from in my hair.

"I'm quite good here, thanks."

I raised an eyebrow. Barsilla sounded a little scared, which was a first for me. I'd always been put in my place by the tiny creature so long as we were in the palace. Here, her voice wavered, and she tightly held my hair.

I was torn. Part of me wanted to rub it in, maybe jokingly hand her over to the spider dude. And the other half of me wanted to show mercy, because even when I get a chance to have vengeance. . . I'm not good at taking it. It took me years to murder my abusive father, and he hurt me daily.

So, I decided not to push the issue.

"Alright, Jello. That's enough," I said, laughing.

To his credit, the spider didn't exactly seem upset with me pushing back. He rubbed one of his mandibles and looked me up and down.

"You must be the queen's new pet I've heard so much about," he said.

"That's me. Werewolf extraordinaire," I said.

He nodded.

"It's almost too difficult to believe. Your kind is so rare that for the queen to have ensnared one. . . I'm impressed," he said.

My. . . kind, I thought. *Aside from Mom, I've never met another like me. And does she even really count? She died when I was a kid.*

All I could do was shrug. Maybe we were rare. But the fact that he wasn't the first fae to mention such a thing did stick out in my mind. The queen had emotional attachments to me. Of that much, I was sure. But to other fae, ones I'd see at Kilgara. . . I'd be a token — no, a specimen.

It'd be like those videos of rich people who own tigers or lions and just let them roam around the house, lying on the couch and shit.

In that case, I'd just have to be all the more threatening to keep their minds off such imagery and more focused on preserving their own lives. Of course, that'd be up to my inner wolf. And I had no doubt she'd be up to the task. Unlike me, she didn't take shit from anybody.

"Well, Jello. If you come by Featherstone when the Raven Queen holds court, you can see my more visceral self on full display," I said. "But until then, I'll ask where we're supposed to go from here."

The spider chuckled and stared into my hair for a few moments. Jello rolled his eyes and pointed to a filthy door covered in dust and mold.

"Out that door, up the cement stairs to your left, and outside by the garage. That'll spit you out onto a path the humans call Free Street," Jello said.

I thanked him, and we left without Barsilla saying a word. Once I'd started up the stairs, she poked her head out next to my ear and said, "Just for the record, in Faerie, his kind prey upon piskies. They find the best hiding spots in the forest and then drop on any little fae that happens to be hovering over the ground, looking for nuts or fruit."

This was a tender confession from the tiny person who'd left me paralyzed on the floor during our first meeting. So, I put all that aside before I spoke.

"I figured it was something like that. But it's not like I would have let him do anything to you," I said.

"Afraid of how your mistress might react?" Barsilla asked.

Shaking my head, I sighed.

"I just know what it's like to be a tiny thing standing before a giant monster that wants nothing more than to hurt you. You try to shrink yourself down so that the monster doesn't see you, but it's never small enough. I always hoped someone would come along when I was trying to shrink myself and snatch me away. So, I guess today I just wanted to be the person that would snatch you to safety," I said, finally spotting a metal door with sunlight streaming in.

Varella's left-hand lady didn't say anything for a moment. But right before we got outside, she spoke.

"That's actually how her majesty found me, you know? I was in the web of someone like Jello, crying out for help. Most faeries ignore such cries since the forest can be filled with them at times. And if you anger a spider, there's always the chance they'll scurry off to a Gohma to have her curse you."

"A Gohma?" I asked.

Barsilla placed both hands on the back of my ear to steady herself as I climbed the last few steps.

"Queens among the spiderlings. Some of them are quite powerful, and once in a while, they'll curse anyone who causes trouble with their underlings. That is, they'll curse anyone. . . except for the ruler of a court. Varella happened to be flying by, heard my cries, and for reasons I've never been able to figure out, plucked me from the web. The spiderling that was savoring me was too frightened to say a word. He just hid under a bush, waiting for the Raven Queen to fly away. I've served her loyally ever since," the piskie said.

Holy shit. Am I bonding with the piskie? I thought, again squashing the temptation to say something mocking of the little fae which could and would get revenge when we returned to Featherstone.

At that moment, Lady Bon-Hwa's words came back to me. She said I craved legitimacy from beings that wore many masks.

Had Barsilla just dropped hers?

"How you felt when she plucked you from the web, Barsilla?" I started. She gripped my ear a little tighter. "That's how I felt the day I struck the bargain with my mistress. Like she'd pulled me out of the jaws of death or something."

I heard the piskie rub her chin.

"So when you submit to the queen, it's about more than a simple pleasure for you. Immense gratitude is also mixed in there somewhere," she said.

Clearing my throat, I felt heat rush to my cheeks. Barsilla was the last person I wanted to discuss submissiveness with. I'd talk about it with Ceras before her. And even they weren't high on the list.

Walking outside, I heard the cries of gulls above us and heard a couple boys laughing as their mother walked by with a shopping bag that said "Remys" on it. Now *that* was a store I remembered. My father dragged me there more times than I could count. And it was always a long haul down to Bangor to visit.

The sky above us was cloudy, and a chilly wind gusted by occasionally, bringing with it smells of a harbor not too far away. A normal person wouldn't smell it from this distance. But I picked up boat fuel and seaweed.

"Do you remember the address?" I asked Barsilla.

"I remember the way from here. The last time I came to the human city of Portland it was through a different pathway. But if you walk down a block and turn left, it'll spit you out on a path called Congress Street."

Doing as I was told, I found myself on what appeared the be the busiest street in downtown Portland. Barsilla guided me with whispers to continue onward past the downtown square where a statue of a large woman stood overlooking dozens of people shopping or visiting restaurants or coming out of the public library.

I read a message on the side that said, "To her sons who died for the Union."

Barsilla whispered, "I've never understood that message. What's the Union? Some kind of human court?"

Sighing and shaking my head, I tried to figure out the easiest way to explain this particularly bloody piece of U.S. history.

"A couple centuries back, this country tore itself in two, mostly over the issue of slavery. What we were taught in school growing up is there was the Confederacy and the Union. People from Maine, that's where we are now, fought for the Union, which tried to put the country back together again."

"Did the Union succeed?"

I nodded.

"They eventually won the war, but a lot of shit happened afterward I don't want to get into. And when I left this place to move into Featherstone — well, let's just say I'd rather live in Faerie than any part of this world," I said.

With the guidance of Varella's left-hand lady, we continued walking down Congress Street for at least a mile before she told me to make a turn. We walked past an old

Italian grocery store, turned again, and finally arrived at a dentist's office.

"Big Smiles? What kind of name is that?" I asked, looking inside.

"The name of a business where mortals go to get their teeth fixed because they don't have glamour to do it for them. Consider yourself fortunate the palace healers make this place unnecessary in Faerie," Barsilla said, tapping on my ear for me to go inside.

Sighing, I did as I was told. . . again.

Unlike most dentist's offices I'd been in, this one was immaculately clean and polished. Behind two receptionists stood a wall covered entirely in ivy. And it was real. I smelled its vegetative scent from where I stood.

To my right stood a glass wall with a water feature running underneath the reflective surface.

A little transparent refrigerator sat next to some uncomfortable wooden chairs, and it was filled with bottled water.

"Hi there!" one of the receptionists said. He appeared to be freshly graduated from college and wore a button-down shirt and black pants. His nametag said "Jace," and had "He/Him" pronouns listed underneath.

"Uh, hi," I said, trying to remember the coded message my mistress taught me before leaving Featherstone. "I need to schedule an appointment as soon as possible. I'm trying to get the shinest teeth in all the land."

I resisted the urge to slap my face in embarrassment. What kind of stupid code was that? This receptionist was just as likely to throw me out as he was to find me a nightmare fae by the name of Dramyra.

Jace snickered a little and said, "Well, who doesn't love shiny teeth? And we've got a great new polishing technique our dentists just started using this month."

An older woman's voice spoke from behind me.

"That won't be necessary, Jace. I'll see her now."

Jace looked surprised.

"Are you sure, Dr. Murphy? I think you've got an appointment in 15," he said.

The voice behind me waved off his concern.

"Just have Melissa take care of that one. This is important."

Jace scratched his wavy brown hair and nodded before punching something into his keyboard. I could only assume he was editing an appointment at the last minute.

When I turned to see who'd been giving orders to the receptionist, I spotted a woman who appeared to be in her early 50s leaning around a corner. She wore a long white jacket and had eyes the color of jasper. As I stared, she blinked horizontally instead of vertically like every other human I'd met.

As my eyes widened, she smiled, and I noticed an inhuman pointedness to her teeth. . . all four rows of them.

"Why don't you come this way, and I'll get you settled?" the fae said.

I gulped and nodded, suddenly getting the heebie-jeebies from this person I was going to follow into a private area.

Dr. Murphy led me past an X-ray closet, a couple rooms with kid-sized dentist seats and small televisions mounted on the roof, and an employee bathroom.

At last, we came to her private office, and she opened the door, motioning for me to enter. When I hesitated, she said, "Oh come now. I wouldn't be so foolish as to harm one hair on the Raven Queen's pet."

Walking inside the surprisingly plain office, I was greeted by a tiny sofa, a mini fridge, a marker board, and a skylight. The walls were painted beige, and a desktop computer sat over in the corner on a screensaver with fish swimming by.

I took a seat on the sofa, and our faerie host closed the door behind us, locking it, which caused me to gulp again.

As soon as the door was closed, the fae dropped her glamor, and before me stood a five-foot-tall woman with pointed ears, turquoise skin, and a shaved head. When she smiled, I saw those four rows of razor teeth and two tongues, one purple, one red.

Her eyes now blinked vertically every few seconds, and they were the color of sand.

Black curled horns hung down from the back of the faerie's skull, wrapping around her ears and ending in spiky white tips.

The faerie leaned against her door and stared down at her claws, which were painted a shade of crimson.

"Dramyra," Barsilla said, flying out from my hair and bowing her head. "It's been some time."

The fae did not seem very impressed at the piskie's sudden appearance.

"Well well. . . if it isn't the Raven Queen's left-hand lady. I don't recall receiving a letter warning of your arrival."

Now I spoke up, bowing my head.

"Apologies. The queen has been busy preparing for a trip to Kilgara. She didn't mean to offend by sending us without an announced arrival," I said.

I shivered when Dramyra's sandy eyes looked me over. It felt like. . . like it wasn't just her eyes watching me, but her shadow's eyes as well. And I didn't like that one bit. She smelled of vetiver and leather. It was a strange combination that seemed to whisper much more was hiding beneath the surface.

"First time seeing a nightara?" Dramyra asked, watching me shiver for the third time in the last hour. It wasn't like the room was cold. Rather, it felt like her glamor kept brushing up against me and light scraping over my arms.

"What's a—" I started, rather stupidly.

Barsilla cut me off.

"Dramyra is a nightmare faerie. Her sister rules the Nightmare Court."

"Well just give her my life story, why don't you, Barsilla?" Dramyra sassed, folding her arms and locking with my eyes.

The room fell silent.

I sure as hell didn't know what to say, so I did what I always did in that situation. . . asked a dumb question.

"Excuse me, Dramyra?"

She smiled at me.

"Yes, royal pet?"

I do not like it when she calls me that, I thought. *In fact, I don't like it when she calls me anything.*

Taking a deep breath as Barsilla turned to flash me a look that said, "Be careful, puppy," I raised an eyebrow.

"My mistress said you lived here in the human world permanently. I was wondering. . . how you survived here in a world of iron and without any glamour?"

Dramyra ran a finger down one of her arms.

"Well, for starters, all of my tools here in the office aren't made of iron. They're custom designed from silver.

Not an ounce of iron here. And I assure you, I have all the glamour I need."

I must have looked like I had more questions because Dramyra pointed a finger at me.

"You must not have a solid grasp on how glamour works. Glamour isn't something that just exists naturally in this world or Faerie. Rather, fae produce glamour by feeding. Different fae feed in different ways. Your queen feeds off your affections as well as the power of her throne. And I. . . well, I feed off the fear of others."

That sounded pretty damn terrifying, which I'm sure was exactly the effect Dramyra must have intended because she just laughed when I slunk down into the couch.

"Oh relax. It's not so bad. I learned a few decades ago that there are some things mortals fear collectively as a species. And one of them?"

It clicked in my head.

"The dentist! I fucking hated visiting the dentist. Growing up, there was no place more terrifying. With every visit, I was petrified that I needed yet another filling or maybe even a root canal."

Dramyra looked pleased with my figuring it out.

"Exactly. So, knowing this, I disguised myself as a dentist, opened this business, and the mortals bring me their terrified children every single day. All I have to do is walk up and down the hall with a mask on my face, looking at paperwork, and nobody suspects a thing. The entire office fills with fear, which I devour, and then I can produce all the glamour I need."

When I realized this, it was kind of ingenious. This was like. . . the ultimate business model for a nightmare fae like Dramyra. And if this place went belly up, she could always disguise herself as an IRS agent. Though that might get her more anger than fear.

Barsilla cleared her throat.

"Oh, yes. You were getting ready to explain why you showed up without warning. Well, go on, little piskie," Dramyra said, her smile fading as she turned her attention back to Varella's left-hand lady.

Pulling out her little clipboard and an even smaller pencil, the piskie looked over a few things as if she was steadying herself for what had to be said.

"Queen Varella is officially calling in her favor. Decades ago, she hid you—"

"I know why I owe her," Dramyra snapped, her sandy eyes glowing orange. "You can skip that part."

Barsilla quickly crossed something off on her papers.

"Right, well, she wants you to make a request to your sister, the Nightmare Queen. Her majesty informed me Queen Trylla will grant you anything you ask of her."

The nightara rubbed her chin as she leaned against the wall even more.

"It's true. My little sister adores me. Though I don't know what the Raven Queen would want from her."

I looked back and forth between the fae, finding myself wondering about how my mistress hid the nightmare fae before me. What were the circumstances? Was it a witness protection kind of thing? Did faeries even have need of that?

It's not like they can call some vacuum store and vanish to Alaska, I thought, scratching the back of my head.

Barsilla looked down at her notes, not meeting Dramyra's eyes when she relayed my mistress' request.

"The Raven Queen wants you to ask your sister for her vote in Kilgara."

Silence filled the room again as I heard Barsilla's tiny heart beating like that of a hummingbird. She was sweating a little, too. But Dramyra's mood changed almost instantly. She laughed louder than I'd heard before and threw her head back.

"Ahahaha! So, Queen Varella is making a move for Bliss. How interesting! Not in a thousand years would I have guessed such a thing. That ought to make for a very interesting summit with the other courts.

Suddenly this mission of great importance made more sense. My mistress sent us to cash in a favor so she could try and stack the deck before we gathered with the other rulers of Faerie to decide who would host Bliss.

The nightara locked eyes with me, and I felt more gooseflesh crawling over my arms and thighs. I really wished she would stop doing that.

"Very well, piskie. I will do as the Raven Queen asks. It's not like I have the power to refuse a favor when I'm in her debt. So you may scurry back with the young wolf here and tell her at least one vote is safely in her corner," Dramyra said. "As for you, Sierra, I hope you're ready to meet folks even scarier than me. And I'd stick real close to that mistress of yours once you leave the halls of Featherstone. You have no idea just how many lords and ladies of Faerie would love to have themselves a pet werewolf. You're quite—"

"Rare," I finished for her. "I've heard it before."

I sounded agitated, but I was just trying to mask my fear. I'd happily submit to my mistress a thousand times. But I was no fool. I knew there were cruel immortals all through Faerie that would find worse ways to hurt me than my father ever could have.

And we were off to a summit where they'd all be gathered.

As we left the dentist, I hoped and prayed my inner wolf had gotten at least a few memories of today and would understand she needed to carry the visage of an absolute killer.

I didn't want to end up in the clutches of a nightara. . . or worse.

CHAPTER TWELVE

Padding through the forest, we were approaching the border of the Raven Court.

The trees around me smelled of squirrels and other creatures that called this realm home I couldn't yet place. I didn't spend much time outside of Featherstone wandering around. In fact, I didn't spend much time outside at all.

It's not that I disliked being free to wander, but I fully understood and appreciated that it was taxing on my inner girl. This body was hers first, and mine second. But as it'd been explained to me, until such a time that we returned to Featherstone, I was to remain present while the inner girl rested.

There were safety issues to consider, and I was the better fighter between us. Though I'd seen scattered memories from the girl showing she was improving, twice now summoning smaller wolves from the darkness to fight alongside her.

Still, the fact remained that it was exceedingly difficult to kill a werewolf.

Varella's voice caused my head to turn as my ears swiveled.

"Remember to be on your guard, my giant wolf. We've just crossed the border of the Raven Court and have entered lands belonging to the Lion Court. Unlike the Worm Court, we share no treaty of mutual aid with our northern neighbors."

Treaties were something I couldn't quite wrap my head around. Bipedal chit-chat on paper is what it sounded like to me. But what I heard from my pack leader as she walked was home is behind us. And the road before us could be hiding enemies at any turn.

We continued our way into the Lion Court, the forest transitioning to wider spaces, still full of trees, albeit different kinds. These weren't trees I was familiar with, but the temperature was climbing steadily, and heat lines wafted over my fur coat, causing me to pant more.

The smells of the Lion Court's southern border were dry grasses and strange beatles I couldn't place. The space between trees continued to widen, which made it easier for the soldiers accompanying us to spread out and have more room.

It was a sizable pack with us today, all armored and carrying their best weapons. As I looked from fae to fae, I saw determination on their faces, as well as wariness. They knew we were vulnerable while traveling so far from Featherstone.

Not long after we left with the soldiers, a memory came to me from the inner girl. She'd asked if the queen wouldn't simply fly us to this place called Kilgara. And the queen's response was this, "Although the courts of Faerie will all meet on neutral and sacred ground for the vote on Bliss, it's still a show of force and power. So instead of flying there in two days, we'll march there in five. And I need the full might of a deadly flock of talons and feathers to show our court is powerful and capable of hosting Bliss."

I could understand at least some of that. She needed the appearance of a strong pack to appear dominant before other fae packs that might seek to challenge anyone with the scent of weakness.

Ahead of us, two fae acted as flag bearers bearing the queen's corvid crest. After more marching, I grew agitated with the pace of our group. Such a large battalion of feathers and talons traveling in formation did not make for an efficient speed.

The queen seemed to sense my frustration, even though I stifled a long groan with a yawn. She walked beside me, patted my back and said, "I know. It's slow going, and you could have been halfway there by now running at full speed. But try to understand, oh giant wolf, that this isn't about merely arriving at the destination. It's about the show that comes with arriving. If my court is to host Bliss, I must show we are powerful enough for such a vast responsibility."

I looked up at her long enough to exchange glances and then turned my eyes back to the path before us, tall golden grass swaying in the breeze as far as the eye could see. Off to my left, a large pond glistened in the afternoon sun. A group of orcs sat on the shore sharpening their weapons and not even turning in our direction. Their gray flesh matched the murky water behind them.

"Of course. . . we may yet have some excitement," the queen said as my ears swiveled and twitched. "No, not them. But I suspect a foolish brigade of mercenaries may try their luck attacking us before we reach Kilgara. Oftentimes rival courts will hire brigands through third parties to attack an enemy on the road. So long as the attack doesn't come on neutral ground, it's a fair strategy."

An attack that might come in the open grassland? That wasn't the type of excitement I was hoping for. A good hunt? Certainly. Throw in a boar running from me at top speed, and I'd be thrilled to run it down. But fae bandits charging out of a hiding spot to ram our party? I saw no sport or fun to be had there.

"You don't seem any happier with this news than you did with our pace, giant wolf. What would it take to sweeten your mood? Your inner girl is simple enough, but with a magnificent beast like yourself, the answer seems like a riddle sealed in a bottle at the bottom of a lake."

I didn't know what the queen expected of me. She knew better than to play the same games with me as she did my inner girl. My purpose wasn't entertainment but protection and threats. Was this simply boredom? Or did she have ulterior motives that were simply beyond my bestial intelligence as a werewolf?

Obviously, I lacked the speech required to answer her verbally, so I just kept walking beside the queen as the day continued.

"Ah, I see it in the way you walk now. Your legs feel stiff. You wish to run loose as your inner girl did a few days ago fleeing the palace. But your duty is here, to me. There is no time to run wild among the grasses and wild cashew trees," she said.

Silence filled the space around us as I sighed and bumped her hip. She swayed but a little. The giant queen heard my message loud and clear, an admission that she was correct in her read.

"Well, you certainly understand your duty, even if it would give way to grumbling in the mouth of someone with the ability to speak," the queen said.

Had I bipedal words to speak, undoubtedly I would be grumbling. But she was right. The pack leader had to be protected, even if the amount of power she possessed made me as her guard somewhat laughable.

Still. . . it was like she said. My presence at her side was part of the show, to her allies, and especially her enemies.

As the sun finally vanished from the sky, my pack leader ordered everyone to make camp. I watched as her feathers and talons unpacked supplies for evening cookies fires and tents. Most of the soldiers had bedrolls they'd been carrying in group chests.

The queen would sleep in a large, private tent with curtains on each side. It was heavily staked into the earth. It'd been a while since I'd gotten to see the moon and stars. Some part of me was looking forward to sleeping under them.

Feathers and talons ate in shifts, and I watched the queen eat with them, telling the soldiers stories of previous marches, some they'd witnessed, others they hadn't. I saw admiration in their eyes. Varella did not hide herself from them but gave herself freely to the faeries that picked up a sword and shield in her name.

Around the fire, they gathered, and the queen led them in a song of the open road.

We've marched for victory day and night.
No trolls or goblins give us fright.
The Raven Queen with all her might,
Will spill fresh blood for our delight.

This song, of course, took into account the queen had both trolls and goblins serving among her ranks, and as soon as the tune was finished, she raised a toast in their name first.

Horns of ale hung high in hands, claws, tentacles, paws, and whatever else the talons and feathers used to hold their drinks.

"My fine talons and feathers, I daresay you are my pride and joy as we march. When I storm into Kilgara to demand our court host Bliss, it will be your splendor and might that fuels my every word," the queen said as everyone laughed and cheered. "So here's to you bastards and bitches that march alongside me. Some of you may not make it home. Hell, I may not make it home. So, in case we find ourselves meeting again over the Silver Bridge, we drink our fill tonight!"

With that toast the fighters of the Raven Court grew more boisterous, yelling, howling, dancing, and living it up in case this was their last night. Of course, we still had a few more nights to go until reaching Kilgara. I wondered if she'd make this same toast each night. And I pondered on what troubles might await us going forward.

At last, my pack leader decided to call it a night. By then, I'd already circled her tent and found an amiable spot where I could both protect her weakest side and still sleep under the stars and moon.

The queen stood, bowed to her feathers and talons (some of whom bowed back and even fell over), and excused herself for the evening. We were to set out exactly one hour after dawn, she commanded.

I found my spot outside of the queen's tent and circled around to bed down when her voice called to me from inside the flap.

"Giant wolf, what exactly do you think you're doing? I don't want you tracking dirt into my bed."

Cocking my head to the side, I just stared into the tent. Only a crack was open, allowing me to see my pack leader's form as she stripped and climbed into bed.

"Well, get in here. Do you expect me to sleep alone in the wilderness? Shall I settle for squeezing a pillow or two as a slumber?"

Yet another moment when I wanted nothing more than bipedal speech to argue. My job was to protect her, and I could do that from out here. It was my first night to sleep in a very long time, and I wanted the night sky above me.

"I am your queen, am I not?" Varella asked.

Sighing, I looked around at the talons and soldiers, any of whom would happily keep the queen company in her bed if she but asked them. Of course, she wasn't asking them. She was asking me, er — commanding me.

Glancing again at my pack leader through the tiny opening of the tent flap, I lowered my ears.

"Good. You acknowledge I am your queen. And I acknowledge that I am a selfish ruler. You wish to sleep under the moon and stars, but I'm not granting that wish," she said with a firm tone just shy of harsh.

Defeated, I wandered into her tent where a bed large enough to accommodate both of us sat next to a table. It was covered in furs and blankets, some of which were pressed against the table containing a pitcher of water and a bowl of fruit.

Incense burned nearby, smelling of lavender, sage, and one or two other herbs that must have been native to Faerie because I didn't recognize them.

The queen was sprawled out in a loose garment for sleeping, head propped up with an elbow. She snapped her fingers, and the tent flap behind me closed and snapped to the ground. Then she patted the bed next to her.

With a sigh, I climbed up on the bed, my paws sinking into its softness. It took all my caution not to accidentally tear something with my claws.

As I circled two or three times and plopped down next to the queen looking away from her, I felt my pack leader wrap her arms around me and pull me tight.

She threw a blanket over the two of us and buried her face in the back of my fur. We lay there like that for a bit in silence, and I heard her speak so quietly you wouldn't even detect her voice from the other side of the mattress.

"I suppose you can know that I'm a little lonely, giant wolf. It's not like you can tell your inner girl what I'm saying, anyway. But. . . I miss her. I didn't use to miss anyone except for my brother, you see. And to have that mortal stumble into my life, tripping and falling into whatever I have in place of a heart. . . well, it's unnerving."

My pack leader's fingers found my muzzle, and she started to run her nails alongside it, brushing my whiskers now and again. Sure, it was no sleeping under the stars. But I'd be a lying wolf if I said it didn't feel pretty damn good.

When she grew tired, the queen yawned and slowly scratched my ears as I heard her eyes drooping behind me.

"You are good company, though, giant wolf. I may not be able to let your inner girl loose out here because of all the danger, but I'll at least sleep easy knowing you'll be in my bed each night with me while we're on the road," she said.

The queen somehow pulled me closer and rested her head above mine.

"You werewolves are remarkable, you know that? I doubt Sierra knows this, but you can only be killed if your head is chopped off, or your heart is pierced with silver. Other than that, you'll bounce back from practically anything," my pack leader said. "Which is good. . . because I intend to keep my pet around for a long, long, long time."

After that, all I heard was the sound of breathing. And I knew she'd gone to sleep. I knew we were formidable beasts. But to the extent it took that much to kill us? That was entirely new to me. And I suppose if my inner girl saw that memory, it would be new to her as well.

With my own eyes growing heavier, and my ears twitching, listening closely to any noises outside my pack leader's tent, I felt satisfied in our safety, in her safety. That was what counted, after all.

And, as much as I hated to admit it. . . I was surprisingly comfortable with the giant faerie queen curled up behind me and soft blankets covering us. Throughout the night, she'd wake up for a few minutes as if afraid I'd left the bed. But when Varella discovered I was still where she'd left me, I'd feel her nails stroking gently behind my ears again.

We went on like that until sunlight started to push against the outside of Varella's tent.

Only four days to go, I thought, yawning in the morning light.

CHAPTER THIRTEEN

The next day started normal. Well, normal as could be in Faerie. It's not like Maine normal back in my previous home up in The County. My pack leader's flag bearers moved forward with the steady march that matched the previous day.

I'd slept better than I thought I would in a mortal bed. Every time my inner girl gave way to me back in the mortal realm, I was usually too busy running around the wilderness to sleep. I'd never gotten the chance to enjoy it. So, although I was looking forward to sleeping under the stars for the first time and was subsequently denied that, it turned out fine.

Part of me wondered if it was because of the queen's glamour pouring over and through me (courtesy of the inner girl's foolish bargain a few months back). Perhaps she was able to lull my restlessness into slumber. It wouldn't be hard. After all, she had a sizable nest of her magic in my wolfheart.

And memories I'd seen of the inner girl with the spy she fawned over taught me the half-fae did the same thing for her each night they shared a bed. A normal human would be flustered and on the edge of anxiety at suddenly having their life uprooted and brought into an unfamiliar world such as Faerie. But having two love interests who consistently steadied the inner girl's heart with their glamour whenever she started to teeter or become afraid was certainly an advantage. At least, from her point of view.

I was just along for the ride, not that this bothered me in the least. The way I saw it, wolves in the mortal realm lived about seven years in the wild. Anything could kill them, disease, starvation, human hunters, bears, rival packs, etc. Werewolves, on the other hand, slept inside a mortal body until the night of the fool moon. And then we tore loose. Almost nothing could kill us. We have no natural predators. And unless the mortal we're bound to ensnares themselves in a fae bargain, we carry few restraints.

The soldiers marched through lunch. My pack leader made a game out of tossing me slices of ham and watching me gobble them before they hit the ground.

I would have been upset at the humiliating display until I considered this was yet another part of the show.

The queen was showing off she didn't just have a legion of soldiers surrounding her on every side, but a speedy, accurate beast with wide jaws that could tear apart almost anything.

Any enemy watching from the woods would see this display and likely back down. It was one thing to be run through with a spear or a blade. You got stabbed and fell to the ground where you'd bleed out. Or if you were lucky, the weapon would take out a vital organ, and you'd die almost instantly with little pain.

But if you fell upon the jaws and claws of a werewolf, there'd be nothing quick or painless about your demise.

That made fae really think about their options before attacking. They were smarter than mortals in that regard because they considered every awful thing that could happen to them. Humans didn't typically stop to consider the threats they faced when out in the world, and even when they did, they were limited by their beliefs of what they might encounter. When you don't believe in immortals lying in the shadows ready to harm you, it gets pretty easy for them to do so.

But fae? They knew what stayed hidden in the shadows. Half the time it was them. And when it wasn't, they were fully aware of what it could be.

"We'll take the northeast path from here," I heard my pack leader yell as my ears twitched from the sudden noise.

Our group gradually switched pathlines and continued at the same frustratingly slow pace, though maybe not quite so frustrating now. The itch and aches were gone from my legs. Had the queen snatched them away with her glamour as I slumbered in her grasp? Was that the cost of losing myself as her claws scratched up and down the back of my neck, bringing every muscle to ease? Likely. Fae bargains crept over every aspect of their society, big and small, realized and unrealized.

I watched a couple hawks fly overhead and noticed the flat grasslands around us were about as open as could be. If something was going to attack, something that would ignore the obvious threat of a werewolf at Varella's side, this would be the place to do it.

And yet, waving golden stalks continued to be all that greeted us for the next while.

With little warning, I felt a chill in the sky, clammy air touching the tips of my whiskers. I came to a dead stop and looked around, smelling moisture and some kind of flowers slowly flooding over the grass. And the flowers did not match the environment we'd spent the last day marching through.

None of what I smelled came from the Lion Court I'd experienced thus far. Varella took immediate notice of my posture and raised a hand. Yet she did not look around. She kept her eyes on me, the faithful canine that sensed an inexplicable change in the air.

But this is what wolves did. It's what we were famous for. Humans so rarely got to see wolves in the wild because we were damn good at sensing the moment something was about to change in our vicinity and either bolting or hiding to attack later.

This was even more true of werewolves.

We didn't just hunt. We knew when something might be hunting us as well. And yet, this feeling I had that caused my fur to bristle didn't seem as though we were being hunted. There was also a hint of a trap we'd stumbled into.

Even my senses couldn't tell when the mist started to creep over the land and surround us. With fish, it was just, one moment they were swimming, and the next they were in a net, ready to become sushi.

But here, with this fog that now obscured my vision and scent on every side, it was as though we'd been walking through it for hours when I knew for a fact it'd only suddenly appeared.

Gradual increments in an instant. That sounded like something perfect for Faerie to have mastered.

Sky, grass, wind, in every direction I looked or smelled, I sensed nothing but this drizzly vapor. The grasslands and wild cashew trees were mostly gone. Tiny pieces remained on the edges of my vision.

If my snout couldn't penetrate the fog, I doubted any fae in our group could. My queen placed a hand on my head and steadied her soldiers.

"Stand sharp, but know this isn't a surprise attack, my feathers, and talons. This. . . is merely a chance meeting along the road. And yet, for all my power as a Faerie queen, I cannot release us from this place. We must instead. . . answer the game," she said.

Everyone kept their hands tight on weapons, though a few eased up their forms and looked around the mist like some answer would appear before their eyes if they just found the right place to stare.

But our new host could not be rushed. Or maybe it was that she simply wouldn't be rushed. Either way, we waited through several tense moments for them to appear, the person who called this fog home.

As suddenly as we were enveloped in this gray moist curtain, she appeared, a tall fae maybe a head shorter than my pack leader. She smelled overwhelmingly of soil and dandelions. Behind her, the little yellow flowers sprang up wherever she walked. Her clothes were sewn together from the pedals of dandelions, what few garments there were. They covered only a little of her green flesh.

She did not appear to contain much glamour, certainly not anywhere as much as Varella. But to envelope an entire squadron of soldiers with mist must have taken quite a bit of magic. Unless. . . she didn't control the clouds and merely followed them, using them to her advantage.

"Well now. More interlopers appear to add to my garden," she said. "This is turning into an interesting day. . . or night. Not that I can tell in all of this."

The fae gestured around to the billowing vapors.

"Teyalla. You know as well as I do that nobody appears in your cage willingly. The prison wanders Faerie, and occasionally you bump into people. Now let us pass."

The flower fae frowned.

"You do not call me by name, Varella of the Dark Wind. I am the ruler of this court, the Dandelion Queen. You will show me proper respect unless you wish to end up in my garden and pass the corvid crown on to that ribbon maiden back in your homeland," Teyalla said with a sneer.

Varella did not appear frightened, but all trace of emotion had vanished from her face as she traded words with this. . . Dandelion Queen.

"Regardless of what you call yourself, you are no queen. And this isn't a court. It's a prison designed to hold you until you willingly shed your immortality and cross the Silver Bridge. A fae cannot be a queen without a people, and all you have are the flowers of your garden," Varella said.

Teyalla appeared her have heard enough.

"If you will not show me the respect I am due in title, then you can join me as my people. Bow to your new queen!" she commanded as a wave of glamour poured over the soldiers.

I felt it simply wash over Varella, but when it hit me, my legs buckled. My desire to kneel intensified. And I felt my willpower crumbling until I heard my pack leader speak words for my ears only.

"Come now, beast. I've not chosen such a weak pet as to wind up in a garden, enslaved to a cowardly fae like this," she said.

Though she stirred no literal power within me, her words were enough that I grabbed hold of an inner rage with my jaws and pulled myself back up with a snarl.

Standing to my full height with fangs bared, I growled at the fae who'd tried to add me to her garden.

"Thatta girl," my pack leader said.

When my mind cleared, I realized that the glamour washing over the legion didn't come from the woman standing before us. It poured out of the mist itself, once again showing me it held the true power here.

The screams of feathers snapped my attention behind as a handful of troops who'd kneeled, knees to the ground, found roots now wrapping around them. They called for the queen to help them, but Varella didn't even look their way.

I started toward them, ready to shred the roots that held each fae, but my pack leader's command stopped me.

"No, no, giant wolf. Leave them be. Their conviction to me waivered, and that's why they fell prey to the whims of a garden-variety fae who fancies herself a queen, ruler in the misty prison. Their consequences are their own," she said, again without a trace of emotion.

The feathers were covered in roots now, and I watched as they began to change shape. They went to the ground on all fours, their skin turning the color of earth, faces flattening inward.

Their arms shriveled, hands turning into leaves. At once, I realized what was happening. Their faces twisted in agony as yellow pedals emerged from the front side of their skull, and their fae features shrank backward into a bulb.

Skin changed to roots and a stem with a constricting vegetative noise. And then they were part of the ground, buried as they shrunk down. Their screams vanished with their size.

In the span of a couple moments, all that remained were dandelions. Those tiny flowers paled the faces of surrounding feathers and talons who took a few steps back.

"There is nowhere for you to sleep, soldiers. Your new queen surrounds you, as does this impenetrable fog. Next time I order you to kneel, know that there will be no sanctuary for you. But fret not. I am not picky. I welcome all to my garden, even disrespectful court rulers that can't be bothered to use proper titles," she said, aquamarine eyes practically burning with animosity toward my pack leader.

Varella's face didn't betray a single thought.

"The rest of us will not kneel, Teyalla. You will let us pass, and we will march to Kilgara. And you will do what you always do. . . bump into wayward kings and queens, snatch a few of their lesser-dedicated soldiers or servants, and be on your way to the next fateful encounter," Varella said.

The Dandelion Queen took a step toward my pack leader, and I stood before her, growling loud enough to shake the flowers around us. Varella smiled.

"You've brought an interesting pet to my garden, Varella. I'd love to see what a werewolf looks like changing into a flower," Teyalla said, eyes now on me.

I did not quiver or shake. I stood my ground, amber eyes locked with her own in an intense glare she broke off.

"Easy, my pet. You cannot kill her. Few can. Only kings and queens of Faerie. Though few are foolish enough to do so. Nobody wants your curse, Teyalla. Nobody wants to trade their actual thrown for the garden of a pretender without a crown on her head."

A cruel smile dotted Teyalla's lips, and I realized there was a maniacal quality to her aura, what little clung to her in the damp air. It came from a prisoner with nothing to lose.

"Do you think my curse a fitting punishment, Varella? Being stuck, never to leave the fog. Carrying around such meager glamour when I used to be a powerful monarch? How long must I pay for my crime?"

My pack leader's eyes were indifferent. She didn't look down upon Teyalla at this moment. The queen merely sounded as though she was reading a sheet of paper with facts written on it.

"That's right. You were a powerful queen. Until two centuries ago you found yourself mysteriously ensconced in inescapable fog. In your temper and impatience, you refused to play the game. You struck down the last Dandelion Queen and became the next one, trapped here until such a time as another brash, impetuous court ruler makes the same mistake," Varella said.

Teyalla advanced, and I did as well. The distance between the meeting of dangers dwindled. I didn't care if she couldn't be killed. I could tear her to pieces and watch those roots put her back together until she couldn't take it anymore.

"You won't strike me down? Fine. Maybe you'll reconsider when I reveal your secret to everyone here. I can't leave this cage, but there are dandelions scattered all over Faerie. Occasionally, I hear things from the flowers as they talk to each other. Irises, in particular, love to gossip, as do toadstools. I know you seek Bliss. And I know why. Shall I reveal it to all who stand before us?"

On the outside, Varella remained calm as ever. But I heard her heart rate tick up a notch and some of the feathers whisper about whatever Teyalla was saying. She held their curiosity. . . some of them.

"Of course, if you kill me here and now, I can't share your secret. Do you want to know what it feels like to be claimed by this curse?" Teyalla asked, cocking her head to the side.

Exasperation covered her face.

"The roots come first, burrowing into your legs so you can't run. They dig into your chest and tear out your heart and glamour, sucking down every last drop. And just before you dissolve, they pump you full of cursed soil that gives you renewed life. . . and chains you to this fog, your glamour, weak as a newborn baby fae. The roots stain your skin green. They leave you smelling of earth and vegetation. And although you're free to take 1,000 steps in any direction, the fog follows. I once commanded an army just as you do now. And at this moment I can nary command even a flower that isn't a dandelion. The mist holds the real power," she said, looking dejected.

I noticed her mask was off, and this was Teyalla's real face. Two-hundred years of wandering the mist with only flowers to keep her company had broken her.

"So come on, Varella. I've suffered enough, haven't I? You've got another queen to manage your court and ensure its future. That's more than most courts have. So release me! Strike me down, and let me go. It's not so bad once you get used to it. You can take prized soldiers from rulers and tempt their tempers. Doesn't that sound fun? Eh, Raven Queen? Shed your crown. Lay down your burdens. Become the Dandelion Queen instead," Teyalla said.

I couldn't tell if this was temptation or pleading. Maybe it was a combination of both.

"No, Teyalla. I will not fall for your ploy. I've no doubt some impetuous ruler will in the future. Maybe tomorrow. Maybe in 1,000 years. But now and again, idiots come to power in Faerie. And this curse serves as a trap to prune them off their thrones. For Faerie doesn't suffer fools for long," the queen said.

Her tone was ice. In it, I heard the caw of a hundred ravens, eyeing a trap with all the wisdom in the world to avoid it.

The Dandelion Queen turned to me once more.

"How about you, beast? Are werewolves not queens among regular and even dire wolves? Strike me down. You want to end my threats toward your mistress, don't you? This is how! Tear out my chest. Let the great earth replace your wolfheart with one made of clay and soil. You'll only regret it for a couple hundred years. And then you can tempt someone else into taking your place."

In that moment I sympathized with her. She was desperate enough to plead with a predator for mercy. Can you imagine a rabbit walking up to a coyote and begging to leap into its jaws? It was madness. But that's what this prison did to the mind of a broken queen.

When I did not move, the Dandelion Queen realized this prison wouldn't be home to me or Varella. It would remain hers until such a time folly granted another monarch residence here.

"You have failed, Teyalla. Tempt another in my place. But not me. Not my pet. Now, let us pass. Three times I've said it, so mote it be. You must stand aside. The game is over," Varella said and ordered everyone to march forward.

They did not hesitate, though I smelled nervousness in the breath of some feathers and at least one talon. For a moment, the Dandelion Queen spoke not. But as Varella walked by her, she said, "May my roots find you one day, Raven Queen. I look forward to clipping your wings."

My pack leader looked Teyalla in the eyes and said with a stone-cold tone, "Keep walking, Dandelion Queen. A crowned moron waits somewhere across Faerie, someone even more foolish than you."

I did not hear a reply. . . unless one counted snarling as such.

We marched until the fog parted and came upon a massive grassy hill. But the land was not Lion Court territory.

Below us stood a valley and a winding path, dotted with fae troops of various banners and courts. The north end of the valley grew densely forested, and my eyes spotted a massive tree the size of half a mountain in the middle of it all.

The wind carried scents of pinewood and oak, as well as glamors of all different kinds, weaving together in a dizzying array. In fact, the valley appeared filled with powerful fae. . . other rulers of this land, surely.

Down there they waited for a meeting that happened but once a century, to decide upon whose court the glory of Bliss would rest.

"My my. It seems the fog did us a favor, shaving off a few more days of travel. Come, my pet. Kilgara awaits."

CHAPTER FOURTEEN

Entering the valley, our legion of feathers and talons was greeted with stares from nobles that'd tagged along after their rulers. The other soldiers and guards, however, stood at attention, not giving our group even an ounce of attention.

Varella walked ahead of a group of soldiers from the Worm Court. They were just one of many spread out across the valley. Yet for all the space we were afforded between the two giant hills, the sheer number of soldiers present from each Faerie court left me feeling stifled.

The valley was full of wild grasses and shrubs. Tents had been pitched for nobles so they could gather and drink and gossip. I spotted flags for the Yellow Court, which I remembered well from our skirmish a few months back.

Fae soldiers were armored in everything from leather to silver to hardened clay and stone. Trolls, orcs, goblins, elves, leonyn, merfolk, chitterin, and many more types of fae stood in formation, waiting for their king or queen to give a command.

We walked past the chitterin legion, which looked like a mix of different insects that were bigger than the average human. I saw fae that looked like mantises, ants, beetles, and hornets all in exoskeletons that looked hard as tree bark and served as living armor. Their limbs and eyes were too numerous to count, and they stood armed with whips, nets, and cruel, jagged daggers.

"The Hive Court. Formidable opponents, and some of the best warriors in all of Faerie," my pack leader said as she caught me staring at them. "You might kill two or three, but eventually the swarm will take you. Many an arrogant general has fallen to them in this way. I've been very careful to avoid their ire during my reign."

I shouldn't have been surprised by this admission. Varella was a powerful queen, yes. But she was wise, as well. And a good leader knows there's always a bigger fish. The best leaders know how to avoid and/or pacify those bigger fish.

Understanding the Raven Court wasn't the strongest queendom in Faerie didn't qualify as enough wisdom to hold the corvid crown. My pack leader knew how to wield the court's strengths and positions to keep its enemies in check, with military might only accounting for some of the solutions.

Looking up at Varella with a wolfish grin, I caught her eyes.

"Whatever could you be thinking at this moment, oh giant wolf? Are you. . . marveling at my political prowess that keeps our home on an even keel with so many potential enemies around us?" she asked, responding with a coy smile of her own.

Maybe I didn't need the ability to speak for her to understand me as she did my inner girl. She was a keen enough read on her own.

I lightly bumped her hip and then returned to wielding a fierce glare for any nobles questioning just how mighty the Raven Queen's pet was.

While I might not be able to kill any foe here, I want them to believe I could, I thought. *Or at least carry enough doubt to hesitate before attacking us.*

After passing the Hive Court, Varella found a relatively open space and told her feathers and talons to stay put. The Raven Court's troops would be sandwiched between the chitterin soldiers and the leonyn fighters of the Lion Court, the mix of bipedal lion warriors and ones that walked on four legs like me, but still spoke the voice of mortals.

The legion seemed to consist mostly of lionesses, but whether they walked on two legs or four, the leonyn troops all wore matching leather armor with a simple crest painted on the rear. The art depicted a roaring lioness, fangs bared and declaring the court's might.

And yet, with all this muscle displayed front and center in the leonyn legion, I got the distinct feeling it was more for show to back down any attackers, rather than an aggressive display to be wielded foolishly.

Whoever leads the Lion Court definitely wouldn't be dumb enough to fall under the curse of the Dandelion Queen, I thought, before pondering what kind of court Teyalla led before striking down the previous flower fae and setting them free.

Varella turned to her feathers and talons before we were completely out of earshot and said, "Be on guard, my warriors. For you are still among fae. But remember not to give in to wanton violence. Kilgara is a sacred space where even the most dreadful fighters dare not shatter centuries of observed neutrality."

Her soldiers answered by snapping even tighter to attention and staring straight ahead. They looked every bit as fierce as the other fighters of Faerie courts scattered throughout the valley.

My pack leader led us further north into the valley toward the forested tip we saw from above. Soldiers grew more sparse as if all the kings and queens of Faerie had acknowledged they were to be left a fair distance from the actual spot where negotiations for Bliss would be held. My paws scraped over a softer meadow, and my fur stood on end as a wave of unfamiliar glamour passed over me.

Looking up at Varella, I wasn't surprised to see her smiling at me. She'd felt it as well.

"No, my pet. That's not me you're feeling. It's the sanctuary we're approaching. Close your eyes and slowly take it in. So few mortals wander into Faerie and even fewer get to see the sacred ground of Kilgara."

We came to a halt so I could close my eyes and do as she instructed. And wolf alive did that energy of this ground we walked on take me for a run.

If Varella's glamour felt like the rush of flapping wings and diving into a moonless night, then the sacred grove we approached was golden sun rays on a lazy day in the field. Waves of grass blew in a breeze that was enough to move each blade but not so strong as to be considered a gust.

In a world of ageless fae, this place still managed to seem ancient. As though kings and queens whose lives stretched across centuries still paused to acknowledge the power of millennia.

The glamour here was one of preservation, as if every fae that passed through here knew not to take any of its power for themselves, nor to pollute it with their magic.

Kilgara was. . . still, even when it was full of soldiers and nobles. They were like dragonflies hovering over a smooth pond, present, but not sending any ripples across the glass-like surface.

When I opened my eyes again with a deep breath, I felt my bones and muscles ease voluntarily. And I understood my queen's last words to her troops. Be on guard because they are still surrounded by opposition courts. But by the gods, don't fuck with this place in any way.

I shuttered to think about the kinds of punishments kings and queens of Faerie would levy upon anyone who dared to violate the neutrality of this site. There was a unique power in a piece of land everyone agreed to respect, even the lowest, most despicable villain seemingly knew to do their shit elsewhere. Anywhere but Kilgara.

"A big staggering, no?" Varella asked.

Our eyes met, and I just stared, not sure I could break the trance. Or maybe I didn't want to. Was I even blinking anymore?

The queen smiled as her violet eyes glowed. I felt her glamour pushing clarity and fierce instinct back into my immediate perspective.

"There's nothing wrong with appreciating the majesty of such a holy place. It was constructed by ancient elven monks some 3,000 years ago. They've all long since crossed over the Silver Bridge, but to this day, the remnants of their sustaining glamour live here, courtesy of the respect and belief from each fae that holds it with reverence in their hearts. . . or even just honors the rule of neutrality."

Varella continued toward the forested part of the valley, and I felt my paws lift and move after her. Though it felt like an out-of-wolf experience for a moment.

"And yet. . . there is always the chance," Varella muttered.

With the forest still a ways off, I noticed painted runes starting to cover the occasional boulder or flat-top rock we'd pass. They glowed with ancient secrets that my wolf mind could shrug off, but I wasn't sure my inner girl would've been able to if she were out.

The grass beneath my paws grew inexplicably softer as we continued, and the first few trees of the forest came into sight. Leaning against one tree was what appeared to be a human-sized raven with bird legs and the arms and hands of a person. Two large black wings rested behind them, starting at their shoulders and draping down to their knees.

"Your grace," they said with what sounded like two voices speaking simultaneously, a man and a woman. There was also a whispering quality to their words as each syllable fled their beak.

Dark feathers covered most of this individual's body, stopping at the neck and allowing for hair the color of mud to flow down between their wings.

The fae now bowing to my queen wore simple blue shorts and a black vest.

Varella nodded at their bow, and they stood against the tree once more.

"Nathoon, tell me what you've learned in the three days I sent you here," she said in a hushed voice.

The ravenfolk bowed again, smaller this time, and gave a quick summary of the last few days. I quickly put together this must be one of the queen's wings, much like my inner girl's other mate, Lily.

"As requested, I intercepted Prince Dareth Ickmunt of the Star Court and bid him return to Featherstone instead of coming here. Though his uncle, the king, already sits in the Kiyawis Grove, along with the other kings and queens of Faerie," Nathoon said.

"I see. Any other arrivals of note?"

"Yes, your grace. Of the 20 recognized courts of Faerie, 17 leaders arrived, now counting yourself. The three absent are the kings of the Court of Games and the Court of Bars, both members of the recent military alliance, the Fist of Kairn, and the Prince of the Never Court, which remains contested due to the pirate conflict," Nathoon said.

The Fist of Kairn. That fucking name again, an alliance of courts causing trouble in northern Faerie. The Prince of Stars came to Varella not long ago pleading for an agreement to accept refugees in the event of invasion. And now my queen had apparently talked the prince into returning to Featherstone instead of reuniting with his uncle, the King of Stars, here.

Sierra didn't have many memories of keeping up with politics in the human world, and I found trying to stay ahead of them here a nuisance. I'd much prefer it if my queen just pointed me at an enemy and said, "Kill." Or pointed to an ally and said, "Don't kill."

But I didn't have the luxury of keeping the intellect of a simple wolf. I had to be the werewolf protector of my pack leader. That was the entire purpose of my being here. And a good protector knows the enemies of those she fights to keep safe.

I have a feeling this Fist of Kairn shit is only going to get worse from here, I thought, looking back and forth between Nathoon and Varella.

"So. . . if the Court of Games and Court of Bars both sat out this gathering, I can only assume the Court of Condors is present in the valley. Though I didn't notice any of their soldiers present in the valley," Varella said, looking back toward where we came from.

I doubted she'd have overlooked any.

"Quite right, my queen. King Kiloona flew here himself, sans army. It caused quite a stir among the nobles who whispered to themselves about everything from the war in the north to the Condor King being the weakest knuckle in the Fist of Kairn."

Varella scoffed.

"Weakness is a perception used to the advantage of many. I do not intend to make that mistake. Showing up in a neutral space while your homeland actively engages in war several courts away tells me he isn't here to seek Bliss. The feeling in my gut just got worse, and I now know I made the right call sending the Star Prince back to my home where Queen Bon-Hwa can protect him."

I exchanged glances with Nathoon's beady eyes that carried more secrets than I had hairs on my body.

"If I may ask, your grace. What does your gut feeling tell you? As far as I've been able to observe, everything in Kilgara appears to be proceeding normally. I haven't detected so much as a snarl between courts that would normally be at each other's throats elsewhere," Nathoon asked.

Suddenly I knew they weren't the same sharpness of spy as Lily. Their mask was looser, and they shed it too easily in the presence of perceived safety. Either Kilgara had gotten to them, or the illusion of safety my queen presented did, and it loosened their tongue.

My pack leader's lips tightened, and all she said was, "The best time to spread trouble is when people perceive safe harbor. Nothing drops a person's guard faster than the belief in the sanctity of tradition. You've done well, Nathoon."

We started for the treeline again, and Varella said one more thing without turning around.

"Stick around, my raven. See what else you can turn up."

I heard them bowing once more, and then we approached what must have been the Kiyawis Grove, sheltered in the nameless trees of old, gnarled bark having witnessed countless ages in a land where time stands still.

The stillness of glamour I sensed only continued to intensify, as if time seemed to move slower around us, even though we continued to walk normally. The way my paws hit the earth appeared to have less of an impact than I was used to. But again, Varella and I moved as we had been without hindrance.

Trees thickened, and I picked up the muted sound of running water, but not from a brook or stream. Rather, the water was flowing from one contained area to another.

I smelled the kings and queens of Faerie before they came into view. Scents of pistachios, piano keys, locusts, bananas, and more filled the air. Each monarch had a distinctive scent that set them apart as a ruling power. A nearly unquestionable authority that permeated their glamour and odor.

Around us, stone statues of druids carrying books and mallets stood still, to mark the legacies of notable elven monks that created Kilgara. Pointed ears, eyes hungry for wisdom, and a sacred sense of discovering how far their curiosity could carry them into the unknown held my focus. These statues were spectacular works of art. I almost didn't have ways to describe the mysticism they carried.

"Come now, my pet. The others are waiting, for we are the last to arrive," Varella said.

Minutes later, we stepped into a grove centered around a massive tree, one big enough to be seen and identified from the top of each surrounding hill.

The tree's bark was ancient, perhaps even older than any of the forest around us, and its roots pulsed heavily with a glamour of the ages. More stone druid statues stood just outside of the tree's reach, armed with hammers and bows. They were once protectors of this sacred land.

Sunlight filtered down through hundreds of branches, each covered with pink and white leaves. And though they blew in the breeze, not a single one fell from the tree. When I looked around, I saw none nearby in the dirt or grass.

A tiny moat filled with crystal-clear water surrounded the tree. Lilypads and tadpoles drifted lazily in the current.

Before us, the tree opened toward the sky, creating a series of walkways and entrances into the heart of the mighty sequoia. Its reddish-brown bark formed a sort of dome that was at least three or four times the size of Varella.

"Welcome, oh giant wolf, to the Kiyawis Grove, the mighty tree of Kilgara. Elven monks once studied under this great tree, meditating to see into the far corners of this world and beyond. It was said the tree itself had roots so deep they reached into other realms, and if you connected with the heart of this grotto, you could see into them."

An archaic stone bridge arced over the tiny moat, allowing Varella and me into the grove. As we stepped under the tree, I put on my dangerous mask. It reminded the queens and kings we saw that the Raven Queen came with a werewolf now, and neither was to be fucked with.

If someone tried to harm Varella, that immortal would meet their mortal end before they could blink.

"Announcing Queen Varella, ruler of the Raven Court at Featherstone, she who soars high above and wields the Dark Wind. And her pet, the Wolf of Featherstone," a man yelled as we entered the tree.

Powerful eyes surrounded us, each monarch sitting on a throne that matched the aesthetic of their home. One remained empty, and it was covered in carvings of dark feathers and crows. The seat contained no precious stones and was only big enough for Varella to sit in. So I lay beside the throne where her nails could just reach the back of my neck, and I could keep an eye on any approaching fools.

"Welcome, wearer of the corvid crown. I trust your journey here was unhindered?" came a sickeningly sweet voice.

Looking over, I spotted him, the Condor King, wearing a silver robe and sandals. He was far from the image of kingly one's mind might conjure. His hair was a brown so dark it might as well have been black, and his eyes were the color of resin, surrounded by rainwater.

His skin was a pale, pinkish hue like uncooked meat in a human market.

"My troops were beset upon by the Dandelion Queen, I'm afraid. But we made it through, sending the gardener on her way. And speaking of troops, King Kiloona, I didn't happen to spot yours in the valley. Will they be joining us in Kilgara at a later time?" Varella asked.

Kiloon's grin left me wanting to vomit on snow.

"I decided my troops were best left at home and came here directly. A once-in-a-century gathering of Faerie rulers left me not wanting to be tardy or waste anyone's time."

Even I could see the barb he'd just lobbed at Varella for arriving last. But her face did not betray any frustration or anger.

"A lovely story to be sure. But wouldn't it be more honest to say your troops were needed for the ongoing invasion up north? Isn't that why your brothers-in-arms aren't joining us? So they can continue to spill fae blood?"

"That's enough, Queen Varella. This council of kings and queens did not travel halfway across our world to mediate a border skirmish to the north," one king said. I turned to look at him and spotted the ruler from the Court of Cheese.

My pack leader had given me descriptions and names of all the rulers she anticipated gathering in Kilgara on the way here. . . before we stumbled into the fog prison.

"King Brie is correct. We're here to discuss the biggest celebration Faerie currently knows. Border skirmishes happen all the time. So let's get to the matter at hand," the Hive Queen said.

With that, silence fell over the gathering of kings and queens. I heard only the sound of running water from the moat outside the giant tree.

"Well, as Queen Dynyra was first to arrive, I propose that she give her proposal for Bliss and start the process for the rest of us," King Yulcifer spoke. The Worm Court king appeared to have lost some weight since last I saw him when his brother had been the cause of an invasion.

Nobody objected, so Queen Dynyra from the Court of Songs cleared her throat and stood to speak. Over the next few hours, she spoke of how much pleasure each fae would have while enjoying the greatest musicians in all of Faerie. Their fabled songs would make for a legendary celebration as radiant glamour from Bliss lit up her queendom.

When she'd finished, King Brie made his proposal for hosting Bliss. As his court was the smallest in Faerie, he had fewer resources to put toward the revel. In fact, everyone seemed to sense this was more of an economic plea to bolster the pockets of wealthy merchants in his home as such a big event was sure to bring travelers who would be carrying considerable coin.

I didn't sense much enthusiasm for anything he said, but rather noticed the general mood of everyone pick up when he was finished talking.

Nobody would vote for the Court of Cheese to host Bliss. One rival down for my queen.

The sun gave way to night during King Brie's proposal, and everyone agreed to take a meal break after he was finished.

Six roasted chickens, nine bowls of strawberries, and seven cuts of steak later, I'd resumed my place at Varella's side.

Negotiations continued, and King Datan of the Yellow Court proceeded to explain how his mighty forces had recently been proven in battle to stand the test of any enemy. King Yulcifer noticeably flinched at this detail, though his former invader did not seem to notice.

"Nowhere in Faerie would your citizens be more safe celebrating Bliss than in my capital city surrounded by Yellow Court soldiers," he said.

When he'd finished, everyone agreed to hear Varella's proposal, and I listened to her heart, which she fought like hell to keep from rattling in her chest.

"My queens and kings. Bliss is a marvelous opportunity, not just for one court, but all courts. And it's in this unity I wish to bring you my proposal. Allow me to organize the greatest revel in centuries, a celebration not just for the Raven Court, but all courts. Instead of everyone traveling to my queendom solely to watch us host Bliss, I'd ask you to allow me to bring pieces of all courts to Perth," she said.

Several heads turned at this suggestion, as instead of giving these rulers reasons why the Raven Court alone was more qualified to host Bliss, she laid out how to best incorporate all courts.

King Brie had, perhaps, the biggest look of shock on his face.

"We all experience the mythic radiance of Bliss upon Faerie, and its majesty belongs to every immortal that calls this world home. No matter where it's celebrated, nobody can guard against anyone else's ability to partake in this splendor. The glamour touches all, servant and queen alike. So why not bring pieces of every court to my own to honor all who will bathe in this ancient glamour? Instead of competing for one court to hold this honor, why not unify and share it equitably among our lands?"

Silence once more fell over the grove. In the distance, I heard nobles and soldiers winding down for the night, preparing their tents and bedrolls. In the forest around us, birds had long since crawled into their nests and silenced their songs.

Varella took the opportunity while everyone was speechless to drive home some of the finer points of her plan, answering questions from kings and queens who were eager to hear how their specialties would be personally invited to this celebration. King Brie and King Yulcifer were especially interested in how their participation in bringing Bliss to Perth could actually be used to honor their own names and courts.

I saw memories from my inner girl of Varella preparing for this very moment with her brother, the Word Sage. And while I can't imagine what his guidance entailed, whatever they'd rehearsed, it fucking worked. She enticed every fae ruler present. All. . . except the Condor King.

He remained silent and even picked at his nails while Varella spoke and answered questions. And yet, she made a point to ignore him, refusing to allow his ignorance to sabotage her moment with malevolence.

In between answering questions, I heard the rulers whispering to themselves as if they'd forgotten a wolf with keen hearing was under the tree.

"Of all the possible proposals, this I did not anticipate."

"She can't be serious. The Raven Queen would be willing to split the glory among us all? Madness. And yet. . ."

"I can't say I'm quite convinced yet. . . but the others sure seem to be."

After her proposal, Varella returned to her throne and resisted wiping her forehead. She placed a sweaty palm down on my head, and I turned upward to lick at her fingers.

Everyone worked through the night and past dawn the next morning. But no king or queen seemed to recapture the group's attention as my pack leader had. My eyes grew heavy and my legs stiff. But these ageless beings didn't seem to want to stop until everyone who'd wanted to speak had done so.

Some of these rulers did love to hear themselves speak. And the more they talked, the more I hated to listen.

When the damn thing finally concluded, everyone agreed to break for lunch before voting. In all, 10 of the monarchs had submitted proposals for hosting Bliss. And as we went to get food, I heard kings and queens in hushed tones speaking mostly about Varella's proposal.

While I tore apart rabbit cutlets, which I thoroughly enjoyed. Rabbits of Faerie were, for the most part, larger and plumper than those in Sierra's previous home.

I also remarked internally on how exhausted my body felt. Werewolves were meant to run free for a night, and I'd been out for a few days now.

My legs ached, and my teeth felt itchy. But I still had a job to do until we reached Featherstone.

Yawning after lunch, I felt Varella's touch upon my neck. She scratched vigorously up and down my spine while I yawned again and felt my muscles springing back to attention.

"Easy now, my pet. This will be over soon, and by tonight, I anticipate we'll be back on our way home."

That sounded good. Then she could pull my inner girl back out, and I could rest for, hopefully, at least a few days. Without Varella using her glamour to call Sierra back, I wasn't sure how long I'd remain like this. Maybe until the next full moon set? I suppose she'd appear at the end of a normal cycle like that. Our body would change back on its own.

But how long was it until the next full moon? A couple of weeks?

Before I could ponder this further, the kings and queens returned to cast their votes. Unlike during the presentation, I heard no frantic heart in the chest of my pack leader. She was calm, almost as calm as the glamour of Kilgara itself.

"Before we cast our votes to decide the host of Bliss, does anyone else wish to speak?" the Hive Queen asked.

Nobody did. It seemed everyone was as eager to return home as I was. Well — everyone except King

Kiloona who just seemed bored with it all. He hadn't made a proposal, and he hadn't asked questions of anyone who did.

To tell the truth, I wasn't even sure why he was here.

His body language said boredom, but memories from my inner girl talking about masks with Lady Bon-Hwa left me doubting that and feeling there must have been something more to his demeanor.

The Condor King was looking up at the tree's canopy above us as everyone cast their votes.

"I vote for Varella," Nightmare Queen Trylla said.

"My vote is also for the Raven Court," the Tulip Court monarch said.

"I cast my vote for myself," King Datan said, looking satisfied with his words.

Humans had some expression about tooting their own horns. That summed up the Yellow Court ruler here today.

"I wish for the corvid crown to have this honor," Queen Dynyra said.

After most of the rulers had voted, all eyes turned to Varella.

"My vote is for Queen Trylla," she said.

Then everyone stared at King Kiloona, who hadn't spoken a word during the vote. He sat sideways on his throne and was picking his teeth with a small animal bone.

"Well, Condor King? What say you?" King Yulcifer asked.

It didn't matter. Queen Varella had all the votes she needed to win, but this was a formality that needed to play out, and this asshole wanted his moment.

"I'll abstain," he said without looking up.

Several of the monarchs scoffed, and the Hive Queen pointed a finger at him.

"You didn't offer a proposal. You didn't bring an army. You didn't ask any questions. Now you're not voting? Why did you even come here, King Kiloona?"

He shrugged.

"All seems pretty pointless to me," he said, eating an apple that appeared as if from nowhere. It made him look like more of an asshole.

More scoffs. Whispers among the kings and queens about this outrageous display. And King Brie spoke up.

"This is the biggest revel in Faerie. It only happens once a century. How can you sit there and call that pointless?" he asked.

At this point, King Kiloona groaned, spit twice after clearing his sinuses, and stood from his throne. His nose was running, and the king didn't seem to care about that either.

"Oh, Bliss isn't pointless. You misunderstand, oh King of Cheese. And, can I say for every ruler here, that is the dumbest title I've ever heard? The Fist of Kairn almost wouldn't even bother invading your shit land if we didn't have designs on reshaping Faerie to our liking."

Nobody spoke now, but many glared. For a prank, this was going too far. Could the Condor King discuss violence on neutral grounds so long as he didn't physically commit harm? What was the punishment for violating this sacred space's neutrality? Could the threatening fae king die as any fae who didn't honor their bargain or oath certainly would?

King Kiloona heaved a great sigh upon the earth and motioned to everyone with a sweeping gesture of his hands.

"You can hold your little vote, gather for your little parties, and honor all the little traditions you outdated lot hold dear. But the hard truth for every court is they will soon be crushed under the Fist of Kairn. What you earlier called a border skirmish will evolve into a full-scale war that consumes all of Faerie. And by the time Bliss rolls around you know who will host? The Fist of Kairn. Because we'll be the only ones left in charge. Er — well, my younger brother and the Court of Games and the Court of Bars will be in charge, anyway."

Varella said not a word, but she stood, and I was instantly beside her growling.

"Featherstone can bring all the little lost puppies and make all the grand unification gestures it wants, but we'll crush it all the same once our troops march south. Of course, we'll take the Court of Stars before then," King Kiloona said, looking over at Prince Dareth's uncle.

Before the King of Stars could retort, the Hive Queen laughed out loud and stood.

"You're three courts, King Kiloona. How do you plan to topple Faerie when the rest of us are unified against you?"

Rubbing his chin, the Condor King held his other arm straight out.

"I'm glad you asked. You see, I figure massive political upheaval from every Faerie ruler being executed at once would be a great place to start. Hard to unify when your successors are scrambling to hold their lands together amid destabilization and chaos."

We all heard a screech, and then a large condor flew into the gathering space under the tree, perching on Kiloona's outstretched arm.

The bird's wings were almost as big as me. Maybe even a little bigger. And the Condor King held it like nothing.

"You came here with no army to a sacred grove of neutrality not even you are foolish enough to violate. How, then, do you plan to systematically execute the rulers of Faerie? Are you going to wait for us all to leave Kilgara and ambush us one by one?" King Brie asked.

Kiloona stopped stroking his bird's feathers and snapped his fingers twice. It then made the most sickening, retching noise and coughed up something into the king's hand. Something black with red on the tip?

The Condor King held his thumb over the red end of whatever he was holding.

"Oh, that's rather simple. I know we all tend to look down on humans for their shortsighted ways and eagerness to bargain away their lives, but the truth is they're pretty inventive for hairy pigs. You see, they spend each day designing new ways to kill each other. Have you heard of this one invention they've made? It's called a bomb. I've got my condors filled with that shit spread all over the valley," Kiloona said.

Varella grimaced and summoned a sword made of dark feathers to her hand. She'd strike down Kiloona if I didn't crush his throat first.

I had a vague conception of what a bomb was, courtesy of memories from my inner girl, mostly from human movies she'd watched now and again with past girlfriends. They went BOOM. Even my wolf brain understood that.

"You're bluffing. Even the maddest king at his highest point of insanity would never resort to bringing human weapons into Faerie," King Yulcifer said. But his heart was pounding, as was King Brie's.

Varella was gritting her teeth, and Kiloona looked right at her.

"Any of you could have killed me by now and stopped this. But none of you will draw blood here because of some fucking tradition of neutrality and sacred spaces. I will wrap those age-old traditions you hold so dear around every neck here, like the heaviest chains you can imagine. Then I'm going to toss those chains into the deepest river so you'll see how pointless they always were and drown, weighed down by the burden of your archaic rules."

My growl began to rattle the tree around us, and I saw Kiloona's eyes widen for a moment.

"You know, Varella. If I wasn't about to die in a fiery hellstorm of iron shrapnel, I might just be afraid of your beast tearing me to pieces. It's a shame she wasn't scary enough to deter me from madness," Kiloona said with a frown that almost seemed legitimate.

"If you try this, you'll die," Varella hissed, taking a step forward with her blade. "By my blade or her fangs, you'll meet a gruesome end, Condor King."

He suddenly looked like the most exhausted soul in the world carrying burdens Kiloona couldn't even begin to describe. And with his eyes, he gazed upon my pack leader's face and said, "I was dead the moment they told me to come here and do this."

Looking around the room as if weighing his last words, Kiloona waved to every monarch, most of whom were standing and now yelling for their guards. But they'd never arrive in time.

"Look me up when we all cross the Silver Bridge," he said, pushing the red button on whatever was in his hand.

Time seemed to slow as Kiloona's condor expanded outward with a deafening noise. Similar echoes came from the valley outside, shockwaves and echoes violating millennia of tradition and sacred upholdings.

But I didn't have time to worry about any of that. With every ounce of speed and strength I had in these precious pieces of a moment, I tackled Varella to the ground. . . hard. I pushed the Raven Queen behind her toppled throne and threw my full body on top of her, all 210 pounds of fur and muscle covering my pack leader as tightly as I could.

The explosion rocketed outward, and for what felt like an eternity all I knew was roaring fire, indescribable flashing heat, and razor blades of iron shrapnel that cut me in ways I couldn't imagine.

CHAPTER FIFTEEN

I'm not sure how long it took me to recover. The people who survived explosions in the movies my inner girl watched didn't seem to deal with too much pain as a result.

Before I blacked out, I remember the hottest flame imaginable, just red-hot molten waves of heat scorching my back. Of course, I'd pressed myself over as much of my pack leader's body as I could. Because I knew if the intense heat didn't kill her, the iron pieces flying out of the fire at high speeds would.

All through my back, ribs, lungs, and heart, I felt jagged iron buried. My skull probably had a piece or two inside as well.

Then there was the force, a shockwave powerful enough to not just break bones but shatter them several times over.

Shields are supposed to be made of wood or metal, not fur, and muscle. But in the piece of a second I had to act, I made my decision and flung myself over Varella.

What was it the Raven Queen had told me as we lay in her bed just a night or two ago?

"You werewolves are remarkable, you know that? I doubt Sierra knows this, but you can only be killed if your head is chopped off, or your heart is pierced with silver. Other than that, you'll bounce back from practically anything," she'd said.

Well, I don't know about bouncing back. When I finally had enough thought in my mind to process pain and damage, I grimaced.

But the fact that I could feel pain meant that at the very least I was alive. Hard to kill indeed.

How long have I been lying here? I thought.

I tried to stand, and while my legs didn't exactly give out on me, they did rip, tear, and burn renewed layers of agony up my hips and spine.

Fuck me, I thought, groaning. *Still, if I can stand, it means my bones have mended themselves.*

Opening my eyes took several minutes. They were buried in ash and scared flesh. When I did finally get them open, none of my visuals made sense. Everything was blurry and distorted. Blinking hurt, just like everything else.

Eventually, I managed to recognize shapes, colors, and patterns.

I listened as my muscles and flesh shifted with a gross squelching noise, pushing the iron shrapnel from my body. Moving two steps to the left was a monstrous feat, but I did it just as the iron fell to the ground with a clanging noise. In total, I think I heard eight or nine pieces hit the ground.

No wonder I was out of commission, I thought, hacking and coughing until another piece of shrapnel ejected itself from my throat with chunks of blood.

My fur felt stiff and matted with blood and ash. The smell of singed hair was enough to make me gag, but I kept my focus.

Stepping back over to my queen, I listened for her heartbeat, placing my ears to her chest. She groaned but did not otherwise speak.

She's alive, I thought, relief flooding my chest. *Smash me 1,000 times, but I need my pack leader to live.*

And yet, she didn't appear to be in good condition. Her left arm and leg were fine because they'd been tucked under me, but her other two limbs were covered in burns, purple and charred black flesh snaking up toward her shoulder.

Her head turned to the side, and I noticed she was covered in my hair. But that was better than being covered in iron.

Speaking of iron, I noticed her neck and the top of her chest were pulsing with some sort of blackened veins. The air was filled with charred. . . well, a lot. But a metallic taste filled everything around me.

Varella coughed violently, her body shaking with every wheeze. Still, she did not stir.

I nosed her cheek, I nibbled on her shoulder, and I sniffed at her ears. Nothing. She remained unconscious.

Even if she survived the blast, I can imagine breathing in all this iron while waiting for me to wake up seared her lungs, I thought. *So long as she remains here, she's being actively poisoned.*

Looking around for someone to help me, I found absolutely nothing.

The massive tree we'd all been talking under just. . . hours or days ago had toppled. A smoke-filled sky above looked down on the pitiful sight that was a charred Varella and her pet werewolf.

Nothing remained of the fae kings and queens that met here. No trace of their glamour hovered in the air.

The water in the moat had evaporated, and all the trees around us were toppled and smoking.

When I closed my eyes, that stillness that made up Kilgara was no more. The glamour of the elven monks who'd made this place had been entirely wiped out. Nothing remained by an impact crater from the bomb of the Condor King.

He'd won. . . killing every single monarch here that didn't bring a pet werewolf to shield them.

Listening for some sign of troops, my stomach dropped to the floor. The valley was deathly silent. No water. No life. No calls for aid or moving of bodies. This was a different kind of stillness, not one made from meditation and lifelong reverence of Faerie and magic, but one devoid of anything resembling life.

Varella coughing again snapped my attention back to her.

I limped back over to her body, which rattled with more hoarse breathing. Her lungs sounded like they were about to burst from her chest. I needed to get her out of this fucking scar of Kilgara before she dissolved to dust like every other fae in this valley.

Nosing at Varella's neck, I nuzzled her for several minutes until she groaned. Her eyes fluttered. But I don't think even now she was truly conscious.

Lying flat against her charred limbs, I barked three times, each louder than the last. She needed to flip over and get on my back.

Barking again, I watched her eyelids twitch some more.

With a heavy groan, she gradually rolled onto her stomach and grabbed my fur with a tiny fraction of strength she'd once used to flip me over and slam me into the earth. This grasp was weak. She was poisoned by iron in the air, and it showed as she visibly shook, pulling herself onto my back.

As she raised herself ever so slightly, I slid underneath the queen. I centered my back under her torso until she was balanced on her canine steed.

Her head turned sideways against my neck and limbs draped limply over my sides, I walked out of the ruined grove.

She bobbed gently with every step I took, and though I wanted to run at full speed to get her out of the valley faster, that just risked her falling off. And if she slid off my back, I wasn't sure she'd have the strength to get back on. Not for a while, at least.

So. . . we carried a steady, careful pace and moved out of the ruined forest and into a valley filled with impact craters. I couldn't even count them all. None of this made sense to me. How had the Condor King summoned so many birds filled with human bombs? Why would he risk this?

Sure, Faerie would be in chaos for a while. But all of these murdered kings and queens had heirs, right? I couldn't imagine they'd take long to form a pack of vengeance and run down the Fist of Kairn into a bloody pit.

Though that wasn't my primary concern right now.

Moving around a boulder that somehow remained intact, though not without crackling and being covered in the dust of what was probably once a squad of chitterin soldiers, I heard Varella moan again.

Hang in there, my queen. I thought. *We're almost to the slope.*

If I needed to exit the valley quickly, I could just dart up the side of the massive hill without worry. But I had precious cargo on my back now.

So, I found a switchback trail and started the ascent, legs popping as more nerves and tendons regenerated. My body was exhausted. Beyond exhausted. I was tired when we arrived at Kilgara. Now? Fatigue was a mark in the dirt I was so far past that it was rendered invisible.

My paws scraped through barren soil, now devoid of glamour and stained with iron residue. But the higher we got, the more the air cleared, and the evidence of the bombs retreated.

It was slow-going. Varella's shoulder bumped into a cliffside, and I had to jump a little to re-center her. She hissed in pain when I did so.

Sorry, your grace, I thought, tongue hanging out of my mouth as I panted. Gods I was tired and thirsty. And I felt like I could eat 20 goats. Werewolves might be able to recover from a bomb blast, but it didn't come without a cost to our scarred, bodies of burnout.

At the top of the hill, I leaned against a tree with withered leaves to catch my breath. The iron in the air had stretched this far. Damn it all.

Varella didn't make a sound, and I panicked for a moment, straining my ears to listen for her heartbeat. It reappeared. . . slowly. Looking back at her drooping limbs, I saw her skin had paled and withered a bit, even on her good arm.

Fuck. . . need to find water fast, I thought.

Smelling the air still brought heavy hints of iron, so I walked back the way we came. After a chunk of the day passed, we'd finally put enough distance between Kilgara and us that I could smell Faerie again, the ageless glamour that ran through the land of mystic creatures and people.

When I sniffed the air again, I finally smelled a stream and started that way.

Water drifted lazily over flat stones, and unfamiliar fish swam along the banks in the shadows of mud towers.

My paws met wet sand, and I lowered my head to drink. . . and drink. . . and drink. Hell, I dunked my whole head in the stream. Gods it felt good. The water was cold and clean.

I took a risk and gently lowered myself into the sand, then rolled Varella over onto her back. She didn't stir. I dove into the stream and came face-to-face with some kind of two-headed turtle that decided to thankfully ignore me.

Taking advantage of the river, I submerged myself several times until most of the dried wolf blood and ash and grime shook free and drifted away in the current, turning parts of the water a brownish red.

When I was finished, I walked back over to Varella, who did not stir. I shook myself dry over her, hoping some of the moisture would wake her up. But she didn't budge.

So, I sighed and walked to the river, sticking my mouth under the water.

Bringing it back, I nosed Varella's neck several times until her mouth opened a little, and I lowered my snout over her lips, letting the water fall loose.

Some splashed over her cheeks, and some ran down her throat. I watched nervously, waiting to see if she'd choke. But she swallowed and seemed to open her mouth for more.

I repeated the process four or five times until she closed her mouth and didn't open it again.

I guess she's had enough, I thought.

My stomach's growl was almost as loud as the one I made toward the Condor King. So, I hunted around the stream until I'd killed a few hares. It wasn't much, but I didn't want to leave Varella alone any longer than I had to.

There wasn't a way for me to make sure she got food, so I ate what I could and then washed my bloodied jaws off in the stream.

My body still carried the aches of a werewolf hit with a bomb, but after a bath, some clean water, and a bit of food, I felt like I had enough strength to carry Varella a little further.

Lowering myself next to her, I nuzzled the Raven Queen's neck until her eyes flickered. She eventually groaned, rolling from her back to her stomach once more as we awkwardly stretched and inched until I was set to carry my pack leader again.

Once she was balanced on my back, I took off down a path in an uncertain direction. It was only a little later when the sun was preparing to set that I realized. . . I had no idea how to return to Featherstone.

Had we traveled straight through the five days north to Kilgara, I could possibly retrace my steps. Though it was a slim chance.

Of course, we didn't come straight to Kilgara. We passed through the fog of the Dandelion Queen before emerging at the once-sacred site.

I had no way of navigating through Faerie, and I was carrying an unconscious, wounded queen. What if I accidentally stumbled into Fist of Kairn territory? Or the land of another hostile court?

On the other paw, what if we found a court friendly to the queen? Perhaps the Star Court? Surely they'd mend her broken body.

There were just too many possibilities, and many of them ended with Varella falling into unfriendly hands.

Fuck! This was all too difficult to deal with on my own. What if I'd just saved my pack leader from a bomb only to lose her to enemies in the forest or a group of bandits?

Growling and lowering my head, I came to suspect my inner girl might think of a solution. But without Varella pulling her out, she was practically unreachable aside from a few shared memories.

I don't know which way to go, Varella. I need help, I thought, lowering my head further and feeling my heart rattling like a jackhammer. I couldn't stay here and wait for the queen to die of iron poisoning. Nor could I take off in a random direction, lest I put us in danger. I had no path.

The goddamn Condor King. . . if he'd just let the meeting conclude, we could have been on our way home right now. And I'd be surrounded by a platoon of soldiers loyal to her majesty.

As fierce as I was. Alone, I just didn't feel enough to save Varella. I'd have given my left ear for Lady Bon-Hwa or Ceras or Barsilla to come flittering out of the bushes with a solution right about now.

I'm alone. . . I thought, sighing and closing my eyes. *I don't know where to go.*

Before I snapped my head back and let out a mournful howl for how fucked I was, my paws started to glow, and I felt glamour stirring within them.

What the fuck? I thought. *What's happening to me?*

That's when I heard a man's voice in my head. An enchantment of some kind called forth a soft-spoken memory from the inner girl. And the man spoke.

"May you always know you are welcome here, young wolf. And in times of need, may your feet find their way to Featherbrooke, a place of rest and solitude."

That's. . . Varella's brother, I thought. *He enchanted my inner girl's feet to always be able to find his home. And he had a way back to the palace!*

It was faint, but I sensed a pull from his glamour, telling me to put the setting sun on my left and advance in that direction.

Raising my tail and feeling like I wasn't alone for the first time in. . . how fucking long had it been since the bomb went off? I had no way of knowing. Let's say the first time in a long time. For the first time since then, I had a direction. No clue how long it'd take me to walk it all. But I'd do it with the Raven Queen tucked safely away on my fur.

The next two days weren't exactly what I'd call easy. I followed the pulsing in my paws that gradually grew stronger.

Ducking between branches and cutting over different trails, even losing the path at one point, I continued.

Working my way over a mountain and cutting across the tip of a tundra. I worried constantly that Varella would freeze. But her heart remained steady.

When we finally made it back into a warmer climate, I noted that her breathing was a little stronger, even though her lungs remained swollen and left her prone to coughing fits that rattled her body.

Maybe the rest and water breaks were helping a little.

On the third day, I was carrying her through a random patch of a jungle we'd stumbled into when I heard a twig snap. My ears twitched, and I realized something had been following us for a while now. But whatever it was remained downwind of me so I couldn't get a lock on its scent.

It didn't take long for five giants to step out of hiding. They weren't exactly quiet this close, and they knew it.

So they revealed themselves and surrounded me. Each was carrying a club with a boulder tied to the end.

"You were right! The she-wolf is carrying the Raven Queen. I'll be damned," one of the giants said.

They were a bit taller than Varella and covered in mossy-green flesh. What little clothing they wore was made from scratchy fur I couldn't even begin to place. But this close, the giant smelled foul, like a mixture of sulfur and mud.

It was their eyes that sickened me the most, though, bulbous, translucent, and filled with some kind of yellow liquid or mucous. The way they swiveled and rotated at odd angles, left me uneasy.

"What should we do with the bitch wolf? Take the queen and try to make it scurry off?"

"No! Take the queen so we can sell her to the King of Games. And then we eat the mangey dog. It's been two days since we had that roach-infested stew. I'm ready for fresh meat!"

"Your mind is full of sawdust, and your tastebuds are the same. Dire wolves taste like shit."

"Well, that's not a dire wolf, though. It's a werewolf. Even bigger, more meat."

"More meat that tastes like shit?"

The giants argued among themselves, and I began to see if there was a way for me to slip by them. But they stopped fighting long enough to block my path.

A giant cleared his nose and then spit.

"Just stay there, bitch wolf. Here is the only bargain you'll get from me. You let us take the queen. And I'll smash you real fast with my club. Easy death. No pain. Then those of us that want to eat shitty meat will. And the rest can. . . I don't know. Go hunting for maggots or something."

I growled. They wouldn't have her. I'd make sure of it. Even if I was outnumbered, these lunatics wouldn't leave the jungle alive.

Humid air permeated a tense situation as the giants looked among themselves. They felt confident enough to win in the end. But none seemed eager to be the first to lose a finger or a hand.

"I don't think she's going to accept your bargain," one of the giants said.

"Then break her fucking legs and jaw," the one who'd offered me that sham of a bargain ordered.

Looking around, I saw a fallen tree that'd been hollowed out and bolted for it. I made it inside just before a club smashed the ground behind me. Letting Varella off my back as fast and gently as I could, I decided to leave her in the log while I picked off the giants one by one from outside.

"Damn it! Now we have to break the log open," one of the giants said before I darted out of the end and sank my teeth into an area he preferred to be treated gently.

His scream of pain filled the jungle as I tore everything loose and charged the next giant. I felt the ground shake as he landed on his back, cursing up a storm.

I did not get a moment of surprise from any of the others. My body was tired and slower than I'd ever felt before. So the fight lasted all of a few slashes, bites, and bashes.

It took everything I had left just to tear one of their hands off, and then one of the giants landed a blow with his club, smashing me into a bush. Before I could recover, another brought his leg down, crashing me into the earth with enough force that I coughed up blood.

They threw me into tree trunks, knocked out a couple of fangs with their clubs, and pounded me with fists the size of truck tires.

And when all was said and done, I was lying next to the hollowed-out tree Varella remained inside.

There were too many ifs running through my mind. If only I hadn't been exploded and carried a body around for three days. If only Varella was awake. If only there were two giants instead of five.

But it all amounted to the same thing, me lying in a puddle of my blood, wheezing because I probably had a few broken bones in my side.

"Well, that ought to have tenderized her meat up nice. Bring your club down on her skull, and let's be done with it. I'm tired of hearing Teeran scream about his missing bits."

One of the giants walked over and raised his club, and I felt my blood run cold. This couldn't be how it ended. Even if this club didn't have any silver in it, I suppose they could tear my head off. But I wasn't really worried about me. I had a queen that I'd been slowly dragging to sanctuary for the last three days. I'd shielded her from a bomb, from iron, from the elements, and. . . and we were going to be done in by a fucking bunch of giants?

No, I thought. *This is the Raven Queen. She welcomed me into her home. She earned my trust and loyalty. She gave my inner girl a reason to smile and hope once more.*

What would my inner girl do when staring down death? I remembered seeing her fight off the lake witch. She tapped into. . . that's it!

Varella had little to no glamour left of her own, but inside my wolfheart was a giant chunk of it. If the inner girl could wield it, then I should be able to as well.

I just. . . needed a way to reach it.

Inside the log, I heard her cough again. She was vulnerable. The Raven Queen needed my help to keep her safe. This is why she'd made me her pet in the first place. My primary role, my number one goal was her protection.

We were beyond threats. We were beyond positioning and shows of strength. Now came the killing moment, me or them. And goddammit, it was going to be them. I just. . . needed her power. It was inside of me. How did my inner girl reach it?!

Varella! I thought, closing my eyes. *I need you!*

Something desperate pulsed through my chest, and I felt it. That ball of glamour she grabbed hold of to pull me out of the girl or the girl out of me. It reverberated through my entire body now as if calling out in response to my need.

Need was my key.

Inside, I pictured my jaws, every tooth I had reaching down into my wolfheart, as far as my neck would allow. And my grasp found the orb of magic from the Raven Queen. When my teeth met that orb, friction dragged it downward. But I held firm. I needed this. She needed this. It was our only way out.

I wasn't sure what this glamour would make of me, just that I needed to become something stronger, something capable of murdering every single one of these giants. I'd become wild and feral if that's what it took.

Each fae carried within them a feral side, a wild instinct that broke into a frenzy in the right circumstances. Here we were at mine.

Raising the glamour inside, I carried it up, up, and up some more until that power pulsed through my very bones. Leaves and tree branches rattled around me. A Dark Wind blew through the jungle. Her wind, her power, living through me.

And the giant that offered me his bargain sensed it. For a moment, I heard doubt in his chest. Something was unsettled as Varella's glamour pulsed within me.

"Now let's see if werewolf tastes better than dire wolf," the giant raising his club said.

By then I was leaping to my feet, dark magic spilling over my body, and instincts going mad. I smelled giant. I tasted giant. I breathed giant. And they would learn the folly of messing with the Raven Queen's pet.

My body changed as Varella's glamour poured out of me. I stood tall and let everything wash over my fur, my muscles, my very being.

With a mighty howl, I unleashed everything. Feathers as dark as midnight poured down my fur, covering every inch of my body and forming a second layer of protection. They were jagged things, eager to cut anything to pieces while keeping me intact.

The club slammed into that outer later and fell into several pieces upon impact.

Before the giant could ask what happened, I vanished from his sight and reappeared, fangs around his throat, using my weight to slam him into the ground.

I tore everything out, and his green blood spilled over the fallen tree. While he twitched, the last bit of life flowing out of him, I bared my fangs at the remaining giants on their feet. They exchanged glances before our fight began again.

The feathers made it easy for me to vanish into shadows and reappear in the blind spots of each giant, tearing off entire limbs with ease. I felt the wind around me in ways I never had before, like my entire body was a giant whisker.

And instead of moving against the breeze, I moved with it for impossible speeds, navigating trees, branches, rocks, and bushes like they were nothing. Obstacles I saw from miles away.

With a roar, I tore down another giant and felt another club fall, sliced into pieces.

My heart was beating like a jackhammer, and adrenaline flooded every ounce of my body as I snapped into a frenzy. My vision narrowed to my targets. Nothing else mattered. I was just here to kill giants, and armed with the power of Varella's Dark Wind, I'd do it with ease.

"Where the fuck did this come from?" one of the giants asked before I tore out his entire knee. On his way to the ground, I felt his fist slam into my side, but the impact dispersed with ease, energy, and force dissipated to the wind.

He screamed and pulled back several mangled knuckles. I ripped the top of his skull open.

More, I thought. *There's still more. And I need it.*

Darting through every shadow and leaving the final giant spinning with terror and a lack of balance, I severed his entire head with my claws.

His surprised expression still showed as that head hit the ground. And while the giant I got the drop on earlier tried to crawl away, pleading for mercy, I made sure to send a simple message from the very queen he'd tried to capture and sell to her enemies.

Touch her and die. Look at her weird and die. Breathe wrong in her general vicinity and die. I am her wolf and deliver the harsh judgment of a dark queen of Faerie. No hesitation. No fear.

I'd thought every giant was dead, but after a few moments, I heard another twig snap behind me. Had I missed one? No matter. My frenzied fangs had strength to burn yet in their mission of unchecked violence. Spinning with a ferocity I was getting more and more attached to every second, I threw myself at this new opponent.

There was a scream. A familiar tone. I'd heard this voice before.

I'd pressed the attacker up against a tree, fangs dripping with drool and blood around a throat, one shaking with terror.

I'd smelled this scent before. Coconut and. . . subtle hints of chamomile.

"Easy now. Easy," she said with narrow breaths and reassurance.

My mind tried to recognize this individual, but the frenzy was so difficult to overcome. I'd worked up an eagerness to kill, to protect my pack leader, and it wouldn't shed for anything so meager as reflection.

"Hey, girl. You know me. Remember? And I know you. Try to focus on my voice," she said.

But my fangs only dug in deeper around her neck. One last obstacle to remove. One final fae to kill, and Varella would be safe. I couldn't stop now.

The girl hissed in pain, and I tasted her blood as drops leaked down the side of her neck. I'd just pierced her skin with my teeth, and a tiny shred of restraint was keeping me from tearing her open.

This blood. . . it was half fae. . . half human.

And then I felt her hands on me, one under my chin, one on the side of my snout.

"I know you're beyond tired. I know you gave yourself into a frenzy and dark glamour to save our queen. And I know you're not going to seriously hurt me, Si. You love me too damn much."

Her glamour was nothing compared to Varella's in terms of power. But there was a queer flavor and gentleness to it that I found myself craving without explanation.

I didn't resist as her glamour gently pushed through me, bringing renewed calm to my mind and tension-filled body.

"You've done so much, little wolf. I'm amazed you made it out here and protected our queen. You slayed giants all by yourself. But it's okay now, Si. You're not alone anymore. I'm here. So, you can put down the dark feathered armor. Set aside the rage. I won't leave you, I promise."

That promise cut right through the fury in my jaws and penetrated my heart. And I was suddenly so fucking fatigued. Dropping the ball of Varella's glamour back into my wolfheart, I heard a loud rustling over me as all the feathers I'd worn fell to the ground and dissolved into a silver dust.

Her name. . . is Lily. She's someone my inner girl loves with all her heart, I thought, releasing her and slowly sitting back down on all fours.

She sank to the ground with me.

"It's okay. You're safe. I've got you, wolf. I've got you," she said.

Slowly, I nosed the shallow wounds where I'd bitten her and licked the blood clean off Lily's neck.

"Relax. You didn't really hurt me. And I knew you wouldn't. Your inner girl is madly in love with me, and she would never allow the big bad wolf to do any serious harm to her Lily."

Lily placed my paws and head in her lap as she stroked my ears, glamour still chasing off bits of frenzy left in my body. Occasionally, my tail would twitch, or my back legs would. And she just eased me into rest with her glamour, just as she did for my inner girl back in Featherstone.

"I'll keep watch over you and the queen, I promise. Just. . . rest for a bit. Your body has been through way more than it ever should have. Easy, girl. Easy."

As my heart rate slowed, I sighed and took her advice. My body slumped, and all the tension I'd carried for three days drained out of me like water in a storm gutter.

CHAPTER SIXTEEN

"Hey, giant wolf. I need you to wake up," a voice said, pulling me from the depths of my exhaustion far before I wanted to stir.

My muscles, my bones, and even my teeth and nails ached as a deep groan rattled up my chest. However long I'd slept, it hadn't been enough to recoup my strength after being blown up and carrying the queen for three days.

Huh. . .what? I thought, bloodshot eyes creaking open.

"I know. I know. But trust me. We need to move," a voice I finally recognized as Lily spoke to me in a hushed whisper. "They're getting closer."

When I didn't stir again, Lily tapped my nose rapidly.

"C'mon, sweetie. Trust me. You deserve to rest for so much longer. But they're coming. Can't you hear them? Drums echoing through the roots and soil?"

My ears and whiskers twitched as I did finally notice the drums beating. I also heard chanting in the distance. Men and women speaking in a language I didn't understand.

I groaned again. It wasn't my active resistance that kept me here. The legs attached to my body weren't responding. They felt like stone lying on the ground, echoes of dull aches that'd remain for days, maybe a week.

Lily's tone grew more hurried. Her heartbeat was steadily picking up the pace, as she no doubt wished I would.

She leaned down to my ears and whispered, glamour stirring from her body to mine.

"In a moment of dire need, with a bond deeper than we know, I, Lily Rootsea, gift my glamour, binding it to your wolfheart. Use its strength to rise once more, oh great wolf. With this gift, my essence, I name you Arreis, the Wolf of Featherstone, and my great love. Arise. Ascend. Awaken."

Her glamour poured through my chest like water inside a glacier and added to a mix that so far seemed to include Varella, Lady Bon-Hwa, and now her. How many more elves could add their glamour to my storage lock of a wolfheart before it exploded like Kilgara?

And yet, for all my grouchiness, I did appreciate the kick of strength her magic added to my body. It wasn't as sweeping as Varella's, but Lily's was still powerful enough to give me a jolt up and at 'em.

No fewer than five joints popped as I rose from the ground, shaking my fur in every direction. Lily put her nose to mine, and I licked her cheek.

"I think Arreis is a pretty clever name," she whispered.

And I think our queen will murder you when she finds out you named her pet, I thought, but could not say to my inner girl's mate.

The drumbeats got louder, and I noticed this time my bones began to ache with their approach. My ears burned with their chanting as their distance decreased.

Lily's skin paled, and her heart raced more than before. Sweat ran down her forehead.

"Listen to me, Arreis. I've infiltrated a lot of places in Faerie, and seen some awful sights, but nothing fills me with more horror than the group approaching us now. They're called the Bone Pickers. They incapacitate their victims with skeletal aches and then, while they're still alive, rip the bones from the body one by one for their personal use," she said, hands shaking.

I looked in the direction of the noise and whined as my legs started to lose their strength granted by Lily's glamour. Dull pain dug into my spine and carried down each limb to my paws.

Lily shook her head.

"We're still several days from the Raven Court. But they've no doubt been tracking you as I did from Kilgara. They don't care about royalty, Arreis. They'll strip Varella's body just the same as yours and mine. Then they'll play their drums using our bones as the sticks and grind our limbs into a powder that they'll mix into white paint that gets smeared all over their eyes and cheeks. We can't fight them. There's gotta be at least 50 in that marching unit alone."

With another whine, I sank to the ground and motioned for Lily to move Varella onto my back in a sitting position.

She started to lay her down when I barked and stayed where I was in the dirt.

"You want me to get on, too? Can you carry two people?" Lily asked.

How did I tell her that I could carry three or four times my body weight and drag twice that much? There was no time.

My joints felt like they were going to shrivel in pain and never return to normal as the drum beats grew louder, and I started to pick up their scents.

They did indeed smell like bone dust and chalk.

With my ears twitching again at the sound of their chants, I barked to Lily once more.

Get on, already! I thought. *I can run faster if you steady the queen.*

My inner girl's mate seemed to understand and slid onto my back behind Varella, holding her steady.

Then I rose and closed my eyes for a moment, trying to get a sense of Vyz's glamour in my paws. It'd been growing stronger, and I had no doubt we were getting closer to his cabin each day.

It snapped to my attention, pulling my head with unmistakable guidance. And I smelled. . .rainwater and swamp.

"Are we too heavy? Do I need to get off?" Lily asked.

Before I could respond that she was being ridiculous, a nude fae with a large drum burst out of the bushes in front of our faces.

His dark blue flesh set him apart from our surroundings, and the fae's eyes were wide with rage and hunger. I met his gaze and saw his entire face smeared with bone-white paint, exactly as Lily had said.

Each of his four hands, two on each wrist, held a bone stick from a creature I couldn't place. But they matched.

The Bone Picker threw his head back, and his long white hair whipped to the ground as he shrieked to summon the others.

"Don't let him hit his drum!" Lily screamed.

Drawing each arm back after the shriek, I felt a pulse of glamour stir within me, the snarling need to remove an obstacle from my path.

With a savage bark that splintered tree back in several directions around me, I saw something shoot out of the ground and wrap around the Bone Picker's wrists just before his sticks made contact with the drum.

He grunted in surprise and cursed in a tongue his partners had been chanting in. When my eyes focused on his restraints, I saw crimson ribbons holding tight. They didn't snap or loosen when the Bone Picker pulled on his restraints.

Lady Bon-Hwa's gift, I thought, still unsure what exactly I'd done. *This glamour shit is enough to spin a wolf's brain around until she can't make heads or tails of anything.*

"Arreis! Go!" Lily yelled, bringing my attention back to the present.

Side-stepping the snared fae, I took off running as the drumbeats and chanting continued behind us. It was a little awkward with two riders, but I was able to move much faster than I had in the past three days.

Lily's glamour kept flowing, so I kept running.

Another shriek rang out into the dark sky behind us, the trapped Bone Picker alerting his unit that we were escaping.

Fortunately, I was faster, and they were upwind of us, so I got a sense of how far we were moving away from them through the night as I followed the pull from Vyz's glamour in my paws.

We continued until I saw the environment open up into a sandy expense in all directions. And across the flat surface, orange rays of sunlight danced in the morning glow.

The smell of rainwater and bog vegetation grew stronger, but I also knew we'd be easier to track leaving a trail in the sand.

"The dried-up lakebed of Amir Gully. Arreis, we need to turn south to return to the Raven Court. Continuing in this direction will just take us into the Storm Swamp."

I ignored her and took off running across the dusty ground.

"Hey, did you hear me? You're heading straight for the Storm Swamp. You need to turn, Arreis."

But I stayed on this track for a while, and she didn't say another word until we were halfway across the lake bed. That's when I suddenly smelled the presence of bone dust and chalk again. A shrieking whistle blew through the air as my ears twitched again in pain.

Lily turned as I kept straight ahead.

"Shit! They sent scouts ahead. They've got skeletal steeds, Arreis. You won't be able to outrun them now that they've entered the lakebed. . . not while carrying us," Lily said.

Fucking watch me, I thought, burning the last of my strength and leaping forward into a full sprint.

My inner girl's mate almost fell backward, but she caught herself and leaned forward with Varella. She dug her hands into my shaggy fur as the wind kicked up, and the sound of thunder filled the air.

Behind us, I started to hear thundering hooves in the dust. But I didn't turn back. I could finally see the swamp ahead of us, a tree line with red maples and water oaks. The wind started to pick up as the ground elevation raised a little with our approach to the former shoreline.

The hooves got closer, but I managed to keep them working hard. I heard hissing behind us as the Bone

Pickers and their steeds pushed with all their might to catch up to us.

Of course, they didn't have to get right next to us. They just had to get close enough and use their flutes to bring us down.

"Arreis, listen to me! I don't know why you won't change course, but the Storm Swamp is no joke. It tears anyone who enters to shreds. Every fae knows this. What you're doing is suicide. Please, turn! If you can run long enough, we might find shelter in the Yarnbottle Caverns due south of here."

I'm not going to run for much longer! I don't have it in me, I thought, panting and feeling exhaustion creeping into my bones. Our only hope was that we make it to that tree line, but I had no way to communicate that to Lily. I just needed her to trust the royal pet.

Of course, unless she hopped off, it wasn't like she had much choice.

A blast of shrill noise brought pain to my teeth, and I growled in response. Their flutes were getting closer.

Lily winced, and I felt her legs tighten around my sides.

We took another hit or two before finally approaching the tree line.

My paws hit damp soil, and a loud clap of thunder drowned out the flutes behind us. Wind raced through my fur, so strong I thought we'd be whipped into a tree trunk.

That's when I felt glamour stirring stronger in my legs, and in a split second, my entire body was glowing with silver aura and driving the wind and water around us as if faerie magic defied the laws of aerodynamics.

Even the thunder was muted, as though I was walking in a dimension between the swamp and the storm.

I finally came to a rest, panting and needing a breather. We turned and saw the skeletal horses charging straight ahead with the Bone Pickers. They must have seen us enter unharmed and felt emboldened. But they soon regretted their choices, all four of them.

Lightning blasted the ground and reduced two of our pursuers to charged corpses and a pile of bones.

The other two were swept up into the wind as though they were plastic shopping bags swirling around a parking lot. The storm slammed them into trees and underwater and over boulders until the blunt force finally killed them.

As Lily had feared for us, the storm quite literally tore them to pieces with unimaginable force.

Still, nothing happened to us as I turned further into the swamp. Barking up at Lily, she finally seemed to understand.

"This glamour protecting you, and by extension us, isn't mine. . .or Varella's. Just how many tricks have you learned in my absence?" Lily asked, raising an eyebrow. I scoffed and started moving us toward Vyzella's cabin.

I stepped over fallen logs and walked around bodies of water that dotted the swamp for several hours until we finally came to a clearing where the storm seemed to stop altogether. It was here I saw a massive Maine coon waiting to greet us.

His fur was a smoky pattern of black, silver, and gray hair that carried centuries of wisdom. Before us was a creature that would cross the Silver Bridge without hesitation the moment his owner did. From my inner girl's memories, I recalled that this particular feline was named Kit.

"I thought I sensed a familiar wolf sniffing around my storm," the cat said with an arrogant charm only cats can pull off. "So this is the mighty werewolf Varella visited with. And speaking of. . .damn, she looks rough."

Kit was stunned into silence for a moment as his eyes looked over Varella's weak breathing and scorched, withered limbs at her side.

"Stars and stones. She's got iron poisoning. You'd better follow me inside quickly. I'll take you to Vyz. He'll know what to do."

And with that, the storm cat led us inside his cabin and up the stairs to where Vyz stood, hands clenching the rail so tight I thought it'd snap under the pressure.

"Var. . .," he gasped as the color drained from his face. The elder brother's silver glamour finally faded around me as my fur returned to normal.

Lily climbed off my back and said, "She's still alive, but barely, Vyzella. I'm sorry to report such terrible news."

He came down the stairs and seemed to flinch upon seeing the Raven Queen's wounds up close.

"How in the nine hells did my sister get iron poisoning? Her lungs are filled with poisonous mortal stone," Vyzella said with some anger clinging to the edge of his voice.

The brother's fists clenched, and Lily cleared her throat softly before speaking.

"She was at Kilgara. I don't know exactly what happened, but the once-sacred valley is covered in stains of iron, fae ash, and craters. Not one soul was left alive in the valley except for your sister. She'd have died if Arreis hadn't gotten her out of the valley. But I don't know what took place during the meeting of kings and queens. And our only conscious witness doesn't speak in a tongue we can understand," Lily said.

Vyz bit his bottom lip, pondering. I wasn't sure what was going through his mind, but his breathing was heavy, and rage pulled at the edge of his eyes.

"Let's get her into a bed. I'll. . .think of something," he said.

Vyz and Lily got The Raven clean and under the covers of her old bedroom here at Featherbrooke. The Word Sage got her to swallow some kind of herbal tea. And for the first time in days, Varella looked a little better. Not much, but a little.

Her breathing was still raspy, as though her lungs might deflate at any second. And Vyz kept touching her forehead and her hands. But there wasn't much else I could do aside from lie on the bed next to Varella and watch him pace, thinking.

My eyes were beyond heavy. I wanted to curl up and sleep. I'd been traveling for days in a body that wasn't meant to be on four legs for longer than 12 hours.

And yet. . .here I was. I wouldn't change back until after the next full moon, not that I was very concerned about it at the moment. All my concern went toward my pack leader, whose life was a little safer here at Featherbrooke than it had been after Kilgara. And yet. . .the Raven Queen had yet to regain consciousness. Her arm and leg were still shriveled and burned. Fever still held her tight without mercy. How close was she to crossing the Silver Bridge? I had no way of knowing.

There are myths that cats can see Death approaching. They see all sorts of things. But wolves' eyes are for the hunt and only the hunt.

After a while of pacing, light from outside seemed to dim, and Vyzella lit the cabin with candles, lanterns, chandeliers, and glowing paint on the walls and ceilings.

Kit finally spoke.

"You know what you have to do, Vyz. You've got to pull the iron out of her and bind it. And if you don't do it in the next few hours, you may become prince consort to the queen-in-command. I know you don't want Bon-Hwa to drag your ass to Featherstone," Kit said.

He spoke with a frankness that would summon wrath or ire in anyone but his deepest friend. Vyzella sighed and crossed his arms.

"She's not strong enough to survive such a spell. Her glamour is practically nonexistent. It's a wonder she hasn't turned to ash like every other faerie in Kilgara. If I attempt to pull the iron out of her, some glamour will come too, and she won't live to wear the corvid crown again."

Kit looked at me.

"What about Sierra? Varella placed a chunk of her glamour inside the girl's wolfheart. If they're touching during the spell, your sister's body will pull what glamour it needs from her pet to survive."

Vyz rubbed his chin and then shook his head after a moment.

"Varella could only do that with Sierra. They share a more powerful bond. Arreis is loyal to my sister, but their bond isn't deep enough for the queen to unconsciously pull glamour out of the wolfheart in this form. We need the inner girl back for the spell to work," the Word Sage said.

Lily placed a cold rag on my pack leader's head, and I found myself wishing I could change back in an instant. That seemed to be the snarl to everything at the moment. I'd done my job in protecting the queen. Now they needed my inner girl to do hers.

Kit broke the silence again.

"Lily, you're obviously connected deeply to Arreis. I smell your glamour on her. Can you change her back?"

The spy shook her head and looked at the ground.

"I'm sorry. I can't. The queen can do it because of her raw magical might, in addition to her connection to Sierra's wolfheart. I'm not powerful enough. And being half-fae doesn't help," she said, placing a hand on my head.

I gently licked her fingers.

We all sat there thinking for a while longer, and Vyz's eyes lit up.

"Lily, I need you to travel to Featherstone and fetch my lover, please. Bring her here," he said.

The wing shook her head.

"It'd take me days to reach Featherstone, and without riding on Affeis, there's no way the storm would allow me back into the swamp."

Vyz gently took her hand and led her over to a snow globe with what appeared to be Featherstone inside of it. He explained to Lily how it worked and sent her off into the glass of what I assumed from seeing my inner girl's memories would take her home.

"I understand you want to be comforted during such a stressful time, but is this really the best time to bring Bon-Hwa here?"

The Word Sage smiled for the first time in hours.

"I'm betting she has the power and connection necessary to pull Sierra out," Vyz said.

And while I wasn't too enthused about the queen in command reaching deep into my wolfheart, my memories told me she'd already done it once to my inner girl. Otherwise, that Bone Picker would've had us.

Lily returned with Lady Bon-Hwa, who examined the Raven Queen with a stern expression. With a sigh, she walked over to me.

My legs popped and groaned as I stood to meet her hand on my head.

"So, it seems we have the royal pet to thank for saving our queen. Her bargain with a foolish mortal girl has paid off after all," she said with a tone that certainly didn't seem to convey much gratitude, even if the words were meant to.

"Can you pull her inner girl out?" Kit asked.

Without turning back to the storm cat, Bon-Hwa said, "Mmmmhhmmm."

She closed her eyes, and I felt the queen in command's glamour probing my chest, looking for a way into my wolfheart. It felt like a serpent slithering through nooks and crannies to arrive at buried treasure.

I wasn't in pain from her efforts, but I did shiver.

"Well, royal pet, I thank you for your great work these last few days, and I return you now to a well-earned rest," she said.

With one last glance at Varella, I sighed and hoped the queen in command knew what she was doing.

I heard Vyz express his gratitude just as I vanished into a cloud of smoke, feeling Bon-Hwa straining and pulling my inner girl to the surface. We passed each other as I closed my eyes and gave way to, at last, welcome rest.

***

As the mist cleared, I fell to all fours, shaking uncontrollably. I felt. . .exhausted in ways I couldn't account for. The strength I clung to as a werewolf was spent several times over. And an unfamiliar hand had brought me back to the world. Well. . . not unfamiliar, just not as familiar as I preferred to reach into my wolfheart.

My vision took a few minutes to clear as the smoke vanished, and my naked body emerged on the floor.

"Wh — where. . .," I started, as my teeth chattered and clicked from my shaking.

Lily appeared from seemingly nowhere and threw a blanket over my body. I blushed furiously upon realizing Lady Bon-Hwa, Vyz, and Kit were present and had now seen me nude.

"Easy, Si. I'm here. You're in Featherbrooke."

Her glamour, which felt much weaker than normal, clung to my shoulders and brought forth a familiar warmth. The warmth of my girlfriend, whom I hadn't seen in weeks.

With what little strength I had, I wrapped my arms tightly around her.

"I'm sorry I didn't have time to bring you a souvenir," she whispered.

My eyes snapped open.

"You got the bird?"

"I got the bird."

"Did it. . . sound normal?"

Lily smiled, and I could tell she was debating something in her mind. She seemed to think better of it and said, "Yup, right up until your message ended. . . suddenly."

I bit my bottom lip.

"Fuck nuggets," I hissed.

My girlfriend giggled.

"It's okay. I thought it was cute, and I got a much-needed laugh from it. Securing Varella's vote for Bliss in the Tulip Court was dull work," Lily said, kissing my cheek.

I felt Vyz's hand on my shoulder.

"I'm so sorry to interrupt your reunion, Sierra. But. . . we have questions. And they're questions only you can answer," he said as Lily helped me stand and steadied me.

Raising an eyebrow and looking around the room, I saw Varella in bed. . . asleep and looking more pale than usual. She had a rag on her forehead.

"Guys. . . what happened?" I started, feeling a tremor in my heart.

Lily told me everything she knew, and Vyz slowly lifted the blanket to reveal the black veins and withered limbs of his sister. My eyes watered, and before I threw myself at the queen, Lady Bon-Hwa caught me.

"Easy now, royal pet. Easy. She's going to be okay. We can cure her iron poisoning. But before we do, you must tell us what your inner wolf saw and heard."

Taking several breaths as the room spun, I had a hard time tearing my thoughts away from my mistress. Lily finally took my face into her hands and gently kissed my forehead, using her glamour to restore a small sense of calm within me.

"Easy, Si. You're okay. She's going to be okay. We've got you. I've got you. So just take a breath and tell us what your inner wolf's memories show you."

With her calm presence inside my mind, I did breathe. . . for what felt like hours.

Then I closed my eyes and greeted the horrors my inner wolf had for me. I saw the betrayal, the explosion, the deaths of every king and queen present at Kilgara, the pain, the chase, the fight, the second chase, and the reason all my strength was drained. It all played out for me in tiny pieces of glass, like each shard contained a clip from a movie. Only the films I watched were her memories. Arreis' memories.

Wait. . . who the fuck is Arreis? I thought, watching my girlfriend name my inner wolf. When my eyes snapped open, I blushed fiercely looking at her.

"Ah, I know which part you just saw," she said, patting my head. "We'll talk about that later."

Indeed we will, I thought.

Leaning on my girlfriend, I took a deep breath and explained everything Arreis had seen and heard, including a word-for-word playback of that fucker, the Condor King.

Vyz ground his teeth. Lily looked at the floor. Kit's tail twitched back and forth. And Lady Bon-Hwa stood still as a statue.

"The Fist of Kairn made their move," she said. "Obviously, they didn't count on the Raven Queen having such a sturdy pet to use as a shield. By the gods, you werewolves are made of steel, grit, and a little wit."

Lily shook her head.

"I never would have predicted them making such a deadly move. They desecrated the sacred grotto! Every court in Faerie is leaderless until successors are named. Most still don't know what happened at Kilgara, or that their rulers are dead," my girlfriend said.

But Vyz walked over to Varella and took her hand. He stared at his younger sister without a word for several minutes. Then, he turned to me.

"I don't think I can thank you enough, Sierra. But I'm afraid we need one more favor from you so I can save my sister's life. All the other political ramifications can be dealt with after your mistress is free from iron poisoning."

Lady Bon-Hwa nodded.

"Well, I've done my part. I'll return to Featherstone and sit the throne until Varella regains her strength. I left

Ceras on the throne as the Raven Ruler in my absence, and gods only know how that's gone to their head."

Before she left, the queen in command pulled me aside.

"Listen to me, royal pet. Even someone as strong as the Raven Queen will need rest after all this turmoil and damage. Normally, I'd want you to keep her here for two weeks. But I know our queen, and she'll push you over like a cardboard cutout. So I'll ask you to keep her here for one week. And then you'll fail at that, easily seduced by your mistress, and return in three to five days. Got it?"

I scowled.

"If I can survive a bomb, I'm pretty sure I can keep our queen on bed rest for a week, Lady Bon-Hwa," I said, crossing my arms.

She ran her nails down the side of my cheek and said, "Listen, young wolf, you melt even locking eyes with her. You fall to pieces when she merely smiles. You are so pathetically weak to her charms that the mortal term of 'bottom' isn't enough to describe you. So when I say you'll struggle to keep her here, believe me. You'll struggle to keep her here."

I fucking hated that she was right, and she loved knowing that.

The queen in command departed but not before sharing a deep kiss with Vyz that left both my eyebrows on top of my skull.

"Meeeeow!" Kit chortled.

After she left, Vyz cleared his throat, smoothed his hair, and said, "Okay, Sierra. Let's heal Var."

CHAPTER SEVENTEEN

Vyzella changed out the rag on top of his sister's forehead. His touch was gentle, as it likely had been all through their lives. Hugs when father didn't care enough, piggyback rides when she started to realize their mother disappeared and wasn't coming back, combing her hair as the young Raven Princess recounted her adventures for the day flying through the forest and counting tree snails, and holding her hand just tight enough when he arrived at the stressful part of any story the Word Sage read to his sister before bed each night.

I saw all of this in the way he looked at her now, wringing out her rag into a bucket and taking the old one away. Kit sat against Vyz's leg.

"It's time," the storm cat said. "She's going to be okay, my friend."

The Word Sage didn't seem to have many syllables and phrases to spare at the moment as his sister's raspy breathing became the main noise in the room. Then, he found his words again.

"She's all the blood family I have left in this world, Kit. How do you live across centuries and somehow wind up with less family than mortals whose days are shorter than the flick of a blade of grass in the swaying breeze?"

Kit looked up at his owner with a slight purr of comfort.

"I could give you the technical answer that it's much more difficult for fae to become pregnant and reproduce despite fucking, on average, more than five times the amount of mortals," Kit said. "But I think the answer you're looking for is more emotional than technical. And as a cat, I much prefer answers of the latter variety."

Shaking my head gently, I just listened to the duo that somehow lived together without pause and never seemed to grow tired of each other's company. Kit and Vyz understood one another through longevity and patience, something few humans would ever obtain, even if they were given twice the time.

The storm cat put a paw on Vyz's leg and said, "You're royalty, my friend. You can hide in the cabin and avoid the crown all day long. But we both know the burden your sister carries for you sitting the throne. She will always be a target for duplicitous faeries that are just doing what comes natural to our species, tricking, scheming, joking, murdering, and a whole bunch of other sly verbs that end in the same three letters."

Kit continued, "The difference now is she has a loyal and rather tough pet to keep her safe. That's why she lies here at this moment, waiting for you to cure her, rather than sitting on the other side of the Silver Bridge, reliving her happiest memories with her brother and awaiting her peaceful dissolution."

Vyz stood and ran his fingers through his hair. The gesture was full of stress and misery.

"I'm not ready to lose her, Kit."

"But you must realize someday you will, my old friend. Or she'll lose you. Because while we call ourselves ageless, immortality isn't absolute, even for us. Deep down, we just use those words to feel superior to the humans that live even shorter lives. The important thing to realize is those things won't happen this day. She breathes, waiting for your strength to pull her back to the living world. So do it."

I took a step toward Vyz and raised my head.

"Word Sage. . . with all due respect, I need you to stop hemming and hawing. Do what you need to for my mistress. . . now."

Silence filled the room, and I realized at once that maybe I'd said something I shouldn't have to Raven royalty. But Kit just laughed.

"Ha! I love this puppy your sister ensnared. You heard her, Vyz. She was more polite than other mortals would have been. Isn't there a phrase where you come from? Stop pussyfooting around? I always figured it had something to do with cats, but I guess not, right?"

I snorted, not expecting the storm cat to use that particular word.

"We can discuss mortal slang when Varella is awake again, Kit. For now—"

Vyz cut me off with a smile.

"For now. . . I'll stop hemming and hawing as you say."

Then he left the room and returned a few minutes later, all smiles gone and a thick tome in his hand. The book, he showed us, was full of blank pages, hundreds of them. Its covers, front and back, were made from thick leather. It looked as though the Word Sage had bound it himself.

"Sierra, take your place in bed with my sister, please. Wrap your arms tightly around her. Her body will need you close to sense the glamour in your wolfheart and pull it in to sustain her."

Looking around the room, I suddenly realized Lady Bon-Hwa had taken Lily back to Featherstone with her. Fair. She's acting queen. I guess my girlfriend had to follow her orders at the moment.

Climbing under the covers and wrapping my arms tightly around Varella's torso, I buried my face in her smooth black hair and smelled her perspiration, practically leaking iron poison from her body. My stomach clenched.

"Hurry," I said.

Vyz nodded, took a few steps toward his sister, and opened the book. His glamour stirred through the room, and I watched his hair rise, eyes glowing violet.

His hands and tongue glowed the brightest as he took a deep breath to begin the incantation.

"We gather here, this day, in my name, Vyzella Tremayne, Prince of the Raven Court. My strength calls upon the Dark Wind. With my words, I stir it around me like a coat of knives."

Covers and loose objects began to whip this way and that in the wind that suddenly filled the room. The bedframe groaned. And I held onto the queen even tighter.

"I am the Word Sage. Tevaka no Ramira Knowlesa. The ageless speech, the mortal speech, every language under the sun and stars is mine to command. I do not use these sentences lightly, so know, so understand that in this moment of dire need, I call you forth, words of the ancients."

The book's pages were rattling in the gale now, and I felt Kit's glamour mix into the storm building around Vyz and Var. The siblings that Death would not break this day.

"By dream or nightmare, we dance through time, spinning riddles, telling tales, dueling valiantly from one moment of passion to the next. We are fae, the immortal ones in the shadow, in the light, nearly always out of sight. This day, my sister's life circles the Silver Bridge, but I call it back. I summon you to return to our living world, Varella, Queen of the Raven Court."

Her body buckled at this call, responding to Vyz's glamour that now pulled at her very essence, fibers that were tainted with mortal stone.

"You are weighed down by cold iron now, but I pull those chains loose from your veins! Come forth, you treacherous poison, and be bound to this tome for all time," he yelled, glamour ripping into Varella's body and tearing the very sickness from her body with all its might.

She coughed and sputtered, but Vyz's magic kept going, pulling out every last droplet of iron. . . and her dwindling glamour along with it.

Her body started to dissolve, and I held tighter.

"No! You can't go now. I won't allow it. Raven Queen, Wielder of the Dark Wind, Caller of my Wolfheart, I refuse to allow you to slip away after all the shit I went through to get you here. Take whatever you need from me. Reach into my very being as you've always done, for I surrender everything to you, my queen," I screamed.

Blinding light tore through the bed, trying to drive us apart, but I used every ounce of strength my body had left to cling tight. No force, not even eternity, would take her from me.

"I need you! You saved my life, you showed me true love, and I'm not ready to let all that go yet. I know you're hurt. I understand that pain weighing you down. But you're the goddamn Raven Queen. And you're my mistress. I love you, Varella," I said, feeling like my arms were going to snap.

As if finally sensing my determination and surrender, Varella's aura dove deep into my wolfheart, grasping at the chunk of glamour she'd buried there.

"Take it. Use it all. Just end this fucking nightmare already!" I yelled, closing my eyes and feeling as though my very soul was being torn at the seams.

And because this wasn't going to end peacefully, Varella's body rose from the bed, hovering in the air. Black feathers appeared around us, darting this way and that. My hair whipped in every direction. But still, I did not let go.

"I bind you iron sickness. I fill every page of this tome with your vehement presence. And I close the book on this cursed chapter once and for all. I, Vyzella Tremayne, Prince of the Raven Court, announce the end!"

With all his strength, the Word Sage slammed shut the tome in his grip, hands burning and smoking with the stench of iron proximity.

Varella's body rocked, rattled, and finally exploded in one final show of glamour that broke the bed into several pieces, blew out the windows, and sent me flying toward the wall.

Closing my eyes and waiting for a sharp impact, I braced myself. But. . . that impact never came. When I gradually opened my eyes, I found a violet gaze staring down at me and the wicked grin of a Raven Queen. Two massive shadowy wings held us in the air without bumping into the ceiling or floor.

And she smelled. . . once more of blackberries and a nighttime breeze, not a hint of iron to be found. I looked down at the arms she carried me in bridal style and found them restored, no burns or withering remained, just a few scars I was sure would fade with proper rest.

"Hi," I said, stupidly.

"Hello, my pet," she said.

"You're. . . back."

She nodded.

"Seems so. I believe you had something to do with that," she said, grin widening.

"Well. . . and Vyz. Oh, and I can't forget Kit and Lily. We all played our parts," I said, still unable to believe my mistress was conscious and breathing again.

My heart swelled with so much joy that it threatened to rupture my arteries and valves with overwhelming force and pressure. I kicked my legs, giddy, as a smirk danced over my lips.

"Sierra Chelsi. You look like you want me to kiss you," she said.

"I'd take a bomb to the face for a smooch from the mighty Raven Queen," I said.

Her infectious laugh returned, and soon her lips met mine.

We landed on the floor of a semi-destroyed bedroom, and Varella set me down while she embraced her brother. He held her tight for several minutes.

"Eloeh t-yrel amho, Var," he said in what I assumed was the ageless tongue.

"Yohar minusa tevala, Vyz," she replied, eyes closed, face buried in his shoulder.

Fuck me. I just couldn't believe she was upright and talking again. Her body still bore signs of exhaustion and battle scars, but the Raven Queen was otherwise alive and well. It'd worked. Vyz's spell had removed the iron poisoning and restored my mistress to the waking world.

"I'm going to go seal this tome away with the other curses in my basement library," Vyz said.

I didn't remember seeing a basement anywhere, but I figured there was a reason for that. You typically kept such things hidden, right?

Kit guided us to a spare bedroom for the two Kilgara survivors to rest. And believe me, rest I intended to do. My inner wolf was doing that in the present. I intended to join her.

Varella and I climbed under the covers of a smaller bed, but still big enough for a seven-foot-tall dark queen of Faerie to snuggle comfortably with her pet werewolf.

The Raven Queen spun me around and made me the little spoon without discussion, and. . . fair. I wasn't going to complain.

Her arms around my bosom, I heard the Raven Queen sigh.

"Thinking about the mess that Faerie is in?" I asked.

She shook her head.

"Thinking about how to deal with the Fist of Kairn?" I asked.

She shook her head once more.

Raising an eyebrow, I pondered what could be running through her mind. Because Faerie was in a political fuckstorm with all its queens and kings dead.

But my mistress surprised me with her actual answer.

"Thinking about the wedding," she said, and I choked on my spit.

"The what?!" I asked. "Whose?"

"Ours. I think you're ready. I'm pretty sure I am. Let's make our binding permanent, Sierra. Being blown to bits has put some things in perspective for me, and I think it's time."

My heart was skipping ALL the beats. I wasn't sure what to say. And she wasn't technically asking me to marry her. Can you tell someone a proposal? Make it an imperative?

"Don't you have bigger matters to worry about right now as the Raven Queen? What about Bliss? And the impending war that'll consume this world?"

My mistress shrugged.

"Those are problems for the sitting Raven Queen to solve. And I've no doubt Lady Bon-Hwa is currently working through them. But at this moment, I'm thinking about a ball. . . maybe a parade. . . something grandiose that announces our permanent union to the world."

I couldn't believe what I was hearing. Was I upset? No. But this wasn't how marriage worked in any of the movies I'd seen.

"Wait. . . if we get married, does that mean I get a promotion? From royal pet to co-queen? I can finally boss Barsilla around! Oh, I can't wait to rub it in her face," I said, giggling with a devilish grin.

But my mistress knew just how to pop that bubble.

"No, darling. You won't be co-queen. When we get married, you'll be my concubine."

I nearly turned to stare at her in disbelief.

"You make it sound like an empty title with no perks whatsoever."

Varella chuckled.

"You don't consider living in the palace under my protection, teasing, gifts, and love a perk?"

"Um, excuse me, mistress, but last I checked, you were under MY protection. I shielded you from the bomb and dragged your unconscious booty back to Featherbrooke, remember? Oh, that's right, you don't. Because you were unconscious. So maybe our positions have reversed. Perhaps now I am the queen, and you are my pet," I said, regretting the words as soon as they were out of my bratty mouth.

For a moment, Varella didn't do anything. And I began to hope beyond all hope that she'd merely fallen asleep and didn't register what I'd said.

"My dear, sweet, naive, soon-to-be concubine. Do you recall the morning when we returned from Featherbrooke?"

My heart sank, and memories of a rather passionate encounter left my core suddenly burning with recalled desire.

"Wh-what about it?" I asked.

"At the height of our fun, when you could've had anything in the world, you asked for what?"

I coughed and lied.

"I'm honestly not sure I remember," I said.

"Oh, well, allow me to remind you," Varella said, rolling me onto my back and snapping her fingers, glamour running over the sheets. I guess she'd really taken most of what was in my wolfheart back into her body.

In my stunned moment of dizziness, I found myself bound, each limb tied by a soft, unbreakable cord to the bedpost.

"You know what, your grace? It's all rushing back to me. I remember now, thanks. You win," I said, horrified that Kit or Vyz might walk in at any moment.

Varella straddled me, every bit of her magnanimous presence restored after a multi-day battle with Death. My heart rate couldn't be measured because it was running so fast.

"Here's what is going to happen, my little submissive werewolf," her voice trailed off.

My mouth was suddenly dry, but I managed to choke out a tiny response. Did she even hear it?

"Y-yeah?" I stammered.

"First, you're going to remember your place in this relationship, not just because of our eternal bargain, but because you cannot get enough of being under me. It leaves you practically begging to be. . . how did you put it at the oasis? Stepped on?"

My face burned as I looked over to the side, unable to meet her domineering gaze.

"Second, you're going to marry me and become my concubine. My power over you will grow to heights you still cannot comprehend as a mortal. And there will be no escape for you, no shelter my influence cannot reach. Consider it a reward for saving my life."

Preparing myself for what we were about to do, I just nodded.

"Yes ma'am."

"Good. And finally. . . Sierra Chelsi," Varella said, as the mark she'd given on the side of my neck dropped several more degrees and sent shivers down my side. "You're going to realize how teasing works. As you spoke arrogantly in your bratty moment, I now leave you bound while I rest on top of you."

She kissed the side of my neck. More shivers. And then she placed her face between my breasts, laid down there atop me, and proceeded to get the rest Lady Bon-Hwa said she'd need.

"What? Seriously? You're joking, right?" I stammered.

But by the sound of her breathing, I knew she was out like a light. And I couldn't move an inch.

"Oh come on! This is beyond cruel, even for you," I yelled. But she didn't stir.

So. . . I sighed and remained put in my place.

Dammit. . . looks like I'm getting married, I thought, as a smile crept over my face again. *There will be pretty dresses and flowers and cake. And I'll be the Raven Queen's bride.*

As the last of Varella's spent glamour faded from the bed top, my bindings disappeared. Of course, with the queen on top of me, it wasn't like I could move.

So I accepted my fate. Pet? Concubine? Eh, fuck it. I was comfy.

ABOUT AUTUMN

Autumn Wolff is a Mainer, bub. And she's a woman of few simple interests. When she's not writing stories about girls kissing each other, Autumn is likely reading stories about girls kissing each other, playing Dungeons and Dragons, riding her bike, or watching a movie. She and her wife live near the ocean and consume more pizza than four turtles mutated by ooze. Autumn may not have the biggest living space, and it may never have enough bookshelves, but it's home.

Twitter: https://twitter.com/AutumnWolff6

Instagram: https://www.instagram.com/autumnwolff11/

Linktree: https://linktr.ee/autumnwolff

OTHER BOOKS BY AUTUMN

Roxie Rivers and the Moonlight Mission - Book Two of the Dream Pack Promises (Coming in July 2023)

Bride of the Elven Innkeeper (Coming in August 2023)

Frigid Harbor (Coming in September 2023)

www.ingramcontent.com/pod-product-compliance
Ingram Content Group UK Ltd.
Pitfield, Milton Keynes, MK11 3LW, UK
UKHW021704190726
13853UKWH00001B/411

9 798852 671776